Pandemonium in Peoria

Boba Book Babes Mysteries Book 1

Rochelle Bradley

CJ Warrant

For all the readers who make author events possible.

Acknowledgments

We would like to thank our beta readers Brandy and Heidi, our editor at Author Services by Kyleigh and cover designer at Pixel Squirrel for making Pandemonium all come together.

Special thanks to our families for putting up with our near-daily FaceTime calls, zoom editing sessions, and for all the encouragement, We love you all.

For the Writers on the River gang... thanks for the inspiration. You've created a monster.

How it all started.

The Pandemonium in Peoria story idea sprouted as Rochelle drove with her boba pal and PA, Brandy, to the Writers on the River author event in Peoria, IL. Rochelle pitched the concept to her "best tea" CJ who immediately started plotting. Thus, the Boba Book Babes mysteries were born.

Boba Book Babes

MYSTERIES

EVERY MURDER HAS A PLOT

CJ Warrant

&

Rochelle Bradley

Pandemonium In Peoria

Chapter 1

Gina

Gina stopped herself from backhanding her twin sister. This wasn't the first time she'd been shoved to the side as Cyndi hustled through a narrow entry. No, the first time had been at birth.

Thank God her boba tea was sealed or there would have been a total mess, followed by a brawl between her and Cyndi.

Gina glanced over her shoulder at Brandy Fuchs, who rolled her eyes. Her friend motioned for Gina to go through the doorway first. She grinned and hurried ahead, eager to get her hard copy map of the book event and the VIP bracelet.

Brandy adjusted her leather book harness while their other friend, Samantha Montgomery, followed, toting a collapsible wagon filled with books for author Rodney Stiff and the cover models to sign. While Brandy focused on the registration table, Sam glanced around tentatively as if the authors or books would bite.

"Don't be afraid. You might like it," Brandy tutted.

Gina shook her head at her friends. Brandy had a bold attitude, whereas Sam was far from a reader and more laid back.

Gina stopped beside Cyndi, nudging her sister in the side with her elbow. She wanted to flip her off, as was their custom, but Gina again restrained the urge.

"Took you long enough," Cyndi teased with a grin.

"And whose fault is that?" Gina snipped, glaring at her twin.

"Name?" an older woman with a blonde bob asked. Her name tag read Barb, and she was the spitting image of Gina and Cyndi's elementary music teacher.

Gina opened her mouth to respond, but Cyndi cut in as usual before she could utter a word. "Cyndi DiCaprio and my sister, Gina DiCaprio."

"That's right." Gina pressed her lips together. She hoped it wouldn't be one of those weekends. She wanted to get along with her sister, but sometimes there were days when being a single child would have been nice.

Barb blinked, then tilted her head in wonderment. "Like the actor?"

"He's our cousin," Gina blurted out the lie for the billionth time.

Smiling, Cyndi stifled a chuckle before she thumbed over her shoulder. "This is Brandy Fuchs and Samantha Montgomery."

"We can talk," Brandy mumbled, smoothing out her periwinkle T-shirt. She'd made them each one featuring a cute boba tea cup, grinning over an open paperback. The words "Boba Book Babes" scrawled over her chest peeked out from under her leather book holster. Rodney Stiff's newest release rested in it on display.

"My sister likes to remind everyone her mouth is the biggest out of the four of us." Gina grinned

"That's what he said." Sam cackled and slapped her thigh.

Gina and Brandy giggled along. Cyndi smirked at each of them. Gina expected her sister to give them a middle finger, but instead, she returned her attention back to the woman.

"Ignore them. They don't get out much." Cyndi stuck her tongue out at the Babes. She took her packet and stepped aside.

The rest of the Babes accepted their packets of information as Barb marked them off the list.

"Ladies, I'm Izzy Drummond. Don't forget to buy your raffle tickets. They'll go on sale right after the panel tonight. All the proceeds will be donated to charity, and the prizes are fabulous," Izzy crooned while she spread her arms and twirled. When she stopped, her pink and blue hair bounced around her face. Colorful unicorn and owl pins lined her blue lanyard strap. "There are book boxes, T-shirts, and gift cards. All kinds of bookish crafts, too, like tablet covers and even handmade quilts. You don't want to miss out."

"Nice." Brandy pointed to Izzy's lanyard. "I like your pins."

"Thanks. I kinda have a thing for unicorns and hooters. Wait until you see my costume for the after-party." She laughed and waved goodbye as another group of attendees approached.

"What's first?" Sam asked, dropping her manilla envelope into the wagon. "Casino? I'm feeling lucky." A tinge of hope coated her words.

Gina and Cyndi's gaze met, and Brandy shook her

head. "You knew what you were getting into, Sam," Brandy huffed.

Sam glanced down at her brown cowgirl boots. "I know."

"Thanks for putting up with our obsession," Gina offered with a smile.

"My reason for coming is to see y'all." Sam grinned.

"And for the tea." Gina winked, then slurped her last boba up the straw.

"I'm glad you're here," Brandy said, weaving an arm around Sam's. She tugged her forward. "Now, come on."

"Let's not forget the gorgeous cover models," Cyndi chimed in. "Especially the one on Rodney Stiff's dragon shifter book or Jamison Blaine's newest m-preg release."

Gina's face heated, but a huge smile broke out. The same hunky hero graced those novel covers and more. It didn't matter if he modeled for sci-fi, paranormal, MC, contemporary romance, or romantic suspense. Clean-shaven or sporting a beard, the man was beautiful. And he happened to be there at the Pandemonium in Peoria author event. She planned to have him sign every book she had with his likeness. She'd even pre-ordered a few he'd modeled for in genres she preferred not to read.

"I want a picture with the models." Brandy smiled like the Cheshire cat. "All of them."

"Mmhmm," Sam hummed. Her gaze circled the convention hallway like a lioness surveying the savanna.

"First things first." Cyndi showed a room on her map. "We need to get to ballroom one."

"I can't wait to see Rodney Stiff again." Brandy took the lead. One wheel of her cart squeaked, although the burgundy carpet muffled the noise.

"I can't believe it's been over three years," Gina admitted as she walked next to Cyndi.

Cyndi side-eyed her sister. "We saw him last year."

"I know. I meant mine and Brandy's friendship. We met in line at Rod Stiff's book signing in Cincinnati." Gina sucked back the last boba and then dropped her empty cup in a trash bin.

He'd been a nobody back then with only one book. Gina and Brandy had stood in line together for forty-five minutes. Polite conversation turned into a deep book discussion, especially over Rodney Stiff's amazing story. But they talked about other authors as well. They exchanged numbers, and the rest was history.

When Cyndi had suggested the Peoria author event, Gina had cringed at the idea. Peoria? Really? The Boba Book Babes had already planned three other events in cool cities, like San Antonio.

Peoria was not on the list of exotic places to visit, even if they had books.

Then, Cyndi had mentioned Rodney Stiff was sponsoring a Friday night panel at the Pandemonium event. Gina had peppered her with questions and then looked up the details on the website. She'd joined the group page and followed the event's social media, but when she noticed Austin Blackmoor, the cover model planned to be in attendance, Gina bought her ticket.

Austin's dark hair, prominent cheekbones, and strong jawline were resemblant of a warrior. With his broad shoulders, toned arms, and a six-pack, Gina would buy and guzzle all books with his likeness.

Meeting him in person would solve one mystery: what color were Austin's eyes? On each cover, they appeared different. He had yellow, reptilian eyes on a dragon shifter book with elongated, vertical pupils. On an MC book, they were a vibrant green.

"Look." Sam pointed to Barb. She was wearing a scowl and had hands on her hips. A pixie-like woman waved her arms as she berated Barb. A red author lanyard hung around the diminutive woman's neck, while another woman with red glasses nodded in agreement.

"That's author Deidra Raines," Cyndi informed.

"Why is she mad?" Brandy asked.

"I don't know. I can't hear them," Cyndi said, slowing down her pace.

They continued forward as the drama unfolded. Deidra pointed across the room toward the panel table. Gina thought Deidra mouthed "Rod Stiff," then she stomped off, leaving Barb glaring in another direction. Gina followed Barb's gaze and froze. Sam ran into her.

"Oh, my God," Gina softly squealed. "There he is."

"Rodney Stiff," Brandy whispered with reverence.

With short dark-blond hair and sun-kissed highlights, the author could have passed as a surfer. But wearing a slim-cut suit with a cobalt tie, he appeared to walk off the cover of a billionaire romance novel.

"Oh, shiitake mushrooms, he's hot." Cyndi fanned herself with the itinerary booklet.

"Tie me up, and call me Sally," Sam hummed. "Forget the models..."

Gina broke out of her trance, pressing forward. "Let's find a seat." *And Austin.*

Brandy snagged a chair and tucked the wagon beside it. Cyndi sat her books and packet next to Brandy's. They helped each other fasten the VIP bracelet around their wrists.

Gina struggled to attach the sticky end of her lavender VIP band.

"Let me," Sam offered as Gina held out her wrist.

"Ooh, there's Addie Werner." Brandy leaned in and lowered her voice as if she was revealing a national secret. "She's one of Rodney's biggest competitors. Her paranormal bear shifter series ranks neck and neck with his dragon shifters."

"I've read the bear series." Cyndi's gaze followed the purple-haired woman as she stepped onto the stage. "You'd like it, Gina. It's a reverse harem. The first book has three men who take one woman as their fated mate."

"I love fated mates." Gina rubbed her chin, making a mental note to add Addie's bear novels to her to-be-read list.

The Boba Book Babes settled into their seats, checking the time. Only a half an hour until the paranormal panel began. Would they talk about shifters, vampires, or other entities? Gina kneaded her hands, anxious and excited to learn about the upcoming releases.

As Gina scanned the platform, Deidra greeted Addie with a hand shake. Smirking, Deidra pointed to Addie's arm. A smile lit Addie's face, and she twisted her arm, showing the other author a tattoo. Gina scrunched her brows, trying to see the colorful design.

A well-dressed man with a yellow lanyard power-walked past them. "Anyone wanting a picture with Rodney Stiff before the panel starts, follow me." He beckoned with a wave.

"Thanks, Harrison," one volunteer stated as she bounced past.

"I want to go talk to Rodney before he speaks." Brandy glanced around another clump of VIP attendees.

"I'll go with you," Gina said. "Hurry, before that group gets to him."

Sam waved them off. "I'll watch the stuff—"

"What if Austin appears?" Cyndi teased, bumping her sister.

Gina grinned. "Oh." She crossed her arms, debating what she should do.

With a smug smile, Sam raised her hand. "I'm for models." Gina high-fived Sam.

"I'll stick with Sam," Gina said, glancing around the room, hoping to spot Austin.

"Then I'm with Brandy." Cyndi stood and left with their friend.

The room thrummed with energy as enthusiastic people, mostly women, flowed into the ballroom. They congregated at the ends of the rows or near the entrance. Some took their seats, studying the map. The noise level rose as the place filled.

Gina observed Barb's interactions with other authors but caught her glowering in Rodney's direction once more.

Deidra and her shadow, most likely her personal assistant, loitered in the back as far away as possible from the man.

Sam poked Gina's shoulder, causing her to jump. "Sorry, but look what just walked in." She pointed to a side entrance where three tall, muscular men in tight T-shirts and skinny jeans stood. As if they inhaled middle-aged readers, a throng of women amassed around them.

Gina climbed on a chair to get a better look. "It's him," she whispered in awe. Austin glanced her way, and they locked gazes. His mouth stopped mid-sentence. A giant smile erupted, and her heart threatened to beat itself out of her chest.

She glanced around disbelieving in a room full of people he smiled specifically at her. Since no one else stood on any chairs, she surmised with hopeful exuberance that Austin Blackmoor's smile was meant for her.

Sam, who didn't need a chair, narrowed her eyes. "What are they handing out?"

Gina hopped down and took her friend's arm. "Let's find out."

They snaked their way over toward the men, who'd been backed against the wall. The models had spread out, and each had a handful of author swag. The bearded red-head handed out signed bookmarks with a breath mint attached. A fan swooned when she held up a Viking romance novel for the model to sign.

Next to him, a buff, wiry but youthful man stood with a lopsided grin. He politely answered questions and flexed while ladies snapped photos. He too was handing out swag of some sort.

Gina skirted the red-head and the baby-faced model, heading straight for Austin's line. She waited, biting her lip as her heart clamored in her chest.

Sam had her phone out, camera mode ready to take pictures.

"He's so tall." Gina sighed.

"Yeah, I think you come up to his belly button." Sam giggled.

Gina stepped on Sam's foot. "Don't make fun of my height."

"Just joking—geez—you better be glad I'm not wearing my good boots," Sam hissed.

Gina ignored her friend's grumblings and peered around the couple in front of them. As she did, Austin glanced up and met her gaze again. The world halted as the oxygen was sucked out of the atmosphere. A slow, sultry smile formed on the model's full lips. How many evenings had she envisioned book heroes in Austin Blackmoor's form, kissing her with those perfect lips and using his tongue in other places on her body? Gina attempted to swallow, but her mouth was like the Sahara.

Sam nudged her, pulling Gina out of her musings. "He is checking you out as if you're biscuits smothered with chocolate gravy."

I wouldn't mind being smothered in his gravy.

The temperature of the room skyrocketed. Gina covered her heart and tried to swallow again. Thankfully, a woman stepped between them and broke the connection. Gina inhaled a deep, calming breath. And another. She studied the shoes of the other VIP guests until she got her heart rate down to semi-normal.

Gina and Sam took a step closer and peered at the man's hands holding lollipops in various colors.

"Gina?" His velvety voice stroked her soul, and her head snapped up.

Mystery solved about his eye color.

Austin's eyes sparkled the color of cinnamon with flecks of gold. They were intense and fascinating at the same time.

She tilted her head, confused. *Austin Blackmoor knows my name.*

"Gina DiCaprio?" he questioned, holding her gaze.

Sam elbowed Gina in the side. She and her friend shared a quick look of shock.

"Hold your horses. How do you know her name?" Sam echoed Gina's thought.

"Please hold these, Molly." Austin handed the lollipops to the woman with red glasses.

Gina glanced at her lanyard and read, *Molly Caudill PA.* She must be Deidra Raines' personal assistant.

Molly reluctantly nodded, accepting the multi-colored sweet treats. A yellow cloth bag with an open book print hung in the crook of her tattooed arm.

Turning his dazzling eyes back to Gina, he asked, "Don't you recognize me?"

"Did Cyndi put you up to this?" *I'll kill my twin, then hug her later.*

"No." A smirk formed on his handsome face. "Are you sure you don't recognize me? After all that time I waited under your bed." One brow rose as he leaned closer. The scent of spice, sandalwood, and soap hit her nose. Gina inhaled, and a shiver ran through her.

Her heart lodged in her throat as she regarded his likeness on the book cover, then studied his face.

It can't be.

It had been over a decade since that night. No one knew what happened except for them, not even her twin.

She shook her head. "It's not possible." But... As she studied his whiskey-colored eyes a bit longer, a familiar memory of a boy she'd crushed on rushed to the forefront of her mind and filled her belly with drunken butterflies. A boy with a different last name.

"It's me, Phillip Moore. You know me as Philly." He grinned and extended his arms. "How about a hug for an old friend?"

"But you're Austin Blackmoor," Gina uttered the denial. She tried to reason how her scrawny first love turned into the hunk of man-meat who wanted to embrace her.

Without further thought, she stepped into his open arms. Surrounded by his warmth, her book crushed between them, her heart hammered, and logic stalled. "I can't believe it's you."

"I want a hug, too," a reader fan spoke up, but Sam shooed them away.

"Who's filly?" Sam asked, tapping her boot.

"Me... We went to school together, and Gina was my first kiss," he said, loosening his grip, but only a little.

"We met in seventh grade when he moved into the area. Phillip from Philadelphia became Philly from Philly." Gina shrugged and pulled away, her face on fire.

Sam pried the book from Gina's locked fingers. "Hot damn. I don't know what you looked like back then, but you're fine now."

"You do look different." Gina sized him up. They used to stand eye to eye at close to five foot four, but now he stood over six feet and she remained the same.

Gina raised her hand, spreading her fingers, and he placed his palm against hers like they used to do. His fingers were no longer the same size and extended at least a knuckle length.

"I was a late bloomer." With a sheepish grin, he laced his fingers with hers. The slide of his warm skin made her mouth dry again. "It's great to see you."

"I can't believe it's you," Gina murmured. Her eyes threatened to fill with happy tears. In all the years, she had never forgotten him or the kiss they shared.

Austin cupped her face, his thumbs skimming her cheeks. Once again, the oxygen had been sucked from her lungs, and Gina found it hard to breathe.

Molly cleared her throat.

The group behind them began to complain. "When is it my turn? I want Austin to touch me too," one fan insisted.

"It's not your turn. Now hush." Sam eyed the basket

and asked, "Um, can I have one of those?" She pointed to the phallus shaped suckers.

"Oh, sure." Austin released Gina and reached into the basket Molly grudgingly held. "What color?"

"Yellow, please." Sam grinned while taking the treat.

"How about you, Gina? What color wanker would you like to suck?" Smirking, he wiggled his eyebrows, and fire ignited in Gina's blood.

"Red is my favorite color," she hummed.

He handed her the sucker. The tip of Gina's tongue licked the corner of her lips, and his smile faltered.

Austin leaned in and whispered. "Hmm. Too bad we're surrounded by readers."

What does he mean by that?

An electronic screech split the air as the sound system boomed. "Fifteen minutes until we begin, folks. Find your seat and prepare to be wowed by the paranormal panel featuring authors Rodney Stiff, Addie Werner, Deidra R..."

The audience cheered as the announcer droned on.

"I guess we need to go," Sam said, tugging on Gina's shirt.

"Hold on a sec." Gina unwrapped the sucker. She noticed Deidra Raines' name had been stamped along the ridge of the stick in bright blue letters. Her gaze drifted to Austin's as she popped the red tip into her mouth.

Austin's mouth dropped open. "C—come find me later."

"Okay," Gina squeaked. Her face ached from smiling. She backed away with a wave, the sucker still in her mouth.

"I'll buy you a drink. We can catch up, and I'll sign the book for you."

"Come on." Sam led the way back to their seats, but Gina stopped her.

"I need to go to the bathroom." What she really needed

was time to compose herself and maybe splash cold water on her face. *Or other places.*

"Okay, but hurry." Sam frowned.

"Look. They won't start without Rodney Stiff." Gina pointed to a slender man holding a black curtain open and motioning for Rodney to exit the stage.

Rodney grimaced at his phone screen, then with one last glance around the room, he slipped out the back.

"Just hurry. I don't want to get grilled by Brandy and Cyndi." Sam plopped onto her seat, her lips tinted a muted yellow.

Gina wove around anxious readers, impeding her escape. Once in the long hallway, she power-walked toward the bathroom but stopped short when Rodney Stiff materialized from the men's room. Holding his purple phone in a death grip, he was furiously texting. His brows dipped, forming a V.

"That greedy little bitch," he growled.

He stomped past Gina without unlocking his gaze from the screen. A hint of sandalwood lingered in his wake.

She remained motionless, monitoring his negative energy, until he pulled open a door to one of the banquet hall's conference rooms and disappeared into the darkness. The author's stormy disposition had almost been enough to make her forget Austin "Philly" Blackmoor. Almost.

Her shoes clicked over the gray marblesque flooring. She proceeded to the handicapped stall. In her mind, she heard Cyndi's voice chastising her. *It doesn't mean mentally handicapped, you doof.*

She opened the next to the last door and then locked it. Sighing, she took a seat. How the hell had little Philly turned into her biggest book boyfriend obsession? She squeezed her eyes shut and breathed, recalling the night before Philly had moved away. His warm lips captured hers in a sweet, mesmerizing kiss. Their love had only begun to blossom. Why had he been uprooted and her life flipped upside down?

The patter of footfalls echoed through the bathroom, returning her to the present. The hushed conversation continued, reaching Gina's ears.

"You shouldn't have said anything," a raspy woman's voice groaned.

"I can't stand his smugness," the other hissed.

"Who does?" Both women laughed. A faucet ran, and words faded in and out.

"It's unbelievable," the nasally woman lamented.

"Everything will be alright. You'll see."

White Mary Janes clacked past. Gina noted a pale blue raindrop tattoo on the right ankle.

"I'm going to kill that SOB and make him pay for what he's done."

Gina's toilet automatically flushed, startling all the women. She stood and smoothed her shirt. When she opened the door a crack, she was alone.

Her phone vibrated with a text. "Where are you?" Cyndi asked with a middle finger emoji. Gina lifted her phone, stuck out her tongue, and snapped a selfie, flipping the bird.

She exited the bathroom and found the hallway deserted. The muffled announcer's voice reminded Gina of Charlie Brown's teacher. A chill crept down Gina's spine, and she rubbed her arms. The eerie vibe persisted as she stepped onto the plush carpet.

A scream tore through the hallway, freezing Gina's blood. She lunged toward the banquet hall's conference room.

Barb, eyes wide with terror, shrieked as if she'd cut her hand off. She clutched her arms tight, hugging herself, shaking.

A pair of shiny black loafers pointed upward. Gina rounded a skirted table littered with swag to find Rodney Stiff. Unblinking eyes stared lifelessly toward the ceiling. His mouth gaped open, with a thin, stubby white stick protruding out from between his lips.

Gina's scream echoed off the wall, forming a duet with Barb's.

Rodney Stiff was dead.

Chapter 2

Austin

"Oh, Austin, can you sign my books?" A fan with bright yellow hair and contacts that reminded me of a lizard boisterously shouted.

"Sure." I took the two novels and started to scroll my name across the inner front page when a chorus of screams grabbed my attention. "Excuse me." I dropped the books into her arms, tore past a throng of fans, and into the hallway.

Past the photographer's set-up screen, a hysterical Barb and wide-eyed Gina, was Rodney Stiff. He was lying on the ground, eyes open, and his mouth agape with something protruding from it.

Needing to make sure Gina was okay first, I reached her side in seconds and pulled her to me. I cupped her cheeks and stared into her watery eyes. "Are you alright?" I studied her ashen face. "What happened?"

"I—I don't know. One second, I was walking out of the bathroom, and the next thing I heard was Barb scream. I went to see what she was yelling about, and I saw..." We both turned in the direction of Rod Stiff's body. "I saw him there—I think he's dead." Gina trembled.

This wasn't how I pictured getting close to Gina. But as I ran both hands along her biceps, trying to soothe her worries, I liked the way she felt in my arms.

"We need to call the police," I said while attempting to pull my phone out of the back pocket of my jeans, but Gina had me in a vice-like grip.

"I called nine one-one." Tammy Shaver, another coordinator for the event, rushed up. She pulled Barb away toward a small group of volunteers who hugged the hysterical, shaking woman.

"Gina, what's going on?" I spotted Gina's not-identical twin sister, Cyndi, closing in, along with two other women who were wearing the same shirts as Gina.

"Cyndi?" She quickly released me and met her sister halfway for a fierce hug, with the others crowded around them. At that moment, my jealousy reared its ugly head. I wanted to be the one to comfort Gina. But as usual, I wasn't worthy of her attention.

Get out of your head. You're not fourteen-years-old anymore.

Letting out a huge exhale, I returned my attention to the dead author. I took a few steps to see if Rodney Stiff was actually dead and not faking it. Three steps toward the body when a loud "stop" echoed off the walls. I spun around as a female officer, dressed in a black uniform, stormed forward.

"Sir, I need you to stay away from the body. It's a live crime scene, and I don't want you to ruin any evidence around the area." She reached my side, glancing my way before checking the body for a pulse. With two fingers to the pulse point on Rod's neck, she announced, "He's dead."

Then the cop proceeded to use the radio cuffed at her shoulder and talked quickly and quietly into it.

After about a minute, she stepped away from the crime scene and took out a notepad. "I'm Officer Anita Cox, and I'm sorry for shouting, but sometimes it's my job. Now, what is your name, and who is this sorry gentleman?"

"Phillip Austin Blackmoor, but friends call me Austin. And that guy is the USA Today bestselling author, Rodney Stiff," I explained while looking around for Gina. She was nowhere in sight, along with her sister and friends.

"So, can you tell me what happened here?" Officer Cox's eyes honed in on my face as though she was ready to catch me in a lie.

"I don't know what happened. I was signing books when I heard screaming, and I ran to see what all the shouting was about when I came upon the scene." I thumbed toward the body.

"Mr. Blackmoor, who's in charge of this event?"

"We are." Barb and Tammy stepped away from the group, hovering close.

"I'm the one who found Rodney Stiff." Barb's eyes were red-rimmed and full of tears.

"You were the only one here to see Mr. Stiff's body?"

Barb wrinkled her nose and closed her eyes for a moment. "No. One of the DiCaprio girls was here." She turned to Tammy. "You know, Leo DiCaprio's cousin."

Tammy rolled her eyes. "I don't believe that for a second."

"Alright then. Can someone find this DiCaprio woman? In the meantime, while we're waiting for my colleagues to arrive, I need the hotel security to cordon off these doors and the areas here." She pointed her fingers at the conference door and the hallway. "Can either of you do that for me? The fewer people loitering around this area would help us."

"I'll take care of that. I'm Josey Wallace, the hotel manager," a short blonde woman said and quickly rushed off.

"So, did any of you see what happened? The killer, perhaps?" She cast a look between Barb, Tammy, and me. Her pen poised millimeters from the paper.

"No. I heard a commotion and saw Mr. Stiff's body lying there. So, I immediately called 911." Tammy's voice shook as she nervously looked at Barb, then began batting her eyes at me.

Jesus. I almost rolled my eyes in annoyance.

"We were calling the headliners up for a VIP panel discussion when Rodney—Mr. Stiff didn't come through the curtain like he planned to do. So, I went to look for him and found him like... this." Barb pointed to the body but quickly folded her arms in on herself. "That's it."

"When did you see this DiCaprio girl? Before or after you saw the body?"

Barb's mouth opened and closed like a fish out of water. "I–I don't remember."

Cox turned to me. "Did you see the DiCaprio girl?"

I slid a look at the body and then back to Cox, who was studying me. I should say yes, I did see Gina here. But something inside me was shouting out; *protect her.*

I was about to tell the cop no when a gravelly voice from behind us stopped me from telling the lie.

"I'm Detective Richard Burns." He flashed his badge like he was some superhero. "I'll take over from here, Officer Cox. Before you start taking names of all who were in this area, why don't you fill me in on what you have." The openly admonished sneer from the female cop to the pretentious rotund man had me step back from Cox, who looked more volatile than the crime scene.

"Pompous asshole." Cox muttered under her breath before she headed to the detective. I guessed this was my one chance to leave and find Gina.

I passed a group of Bradley Prince fans who had crocheted creatures as hats, asking them if they saw four women with boba T-shirts. They shook their heads but pointed in the direction of the main room where the signing was going to take place. Possibly not now, with Rodney's death.

Did the officer say it was murder? I wasn't sure. I rubbed my head, not believing such things could happen at a book event like this. No matter. Gina was my first priority. I needed to know if she was okay. Then, I'd ask what she knew about Rodney's death.

I checked the signing room, but no luck. Apparently, Gina and her gang disappeared. Maybe they'd gone to the riverboat casino or outside for some fresh air, but with the rest of the police brigade here, the girls might have been hustled back inside. A tinge of worry raced up my spine as I quickly looked out the front lobby doors. Not a single civilian in sight, other than squad cars, uniformed cops, and a reporter with her camera crew standing by the entrance.

"Philly." I turned, and a rush of warmth and relief flooded through me at the sight of Gina's face. "Sorry, Austin. I couldn't stand there any longer. His lifeless eyes were freaking me out."

"You're okay?" I asked, longing to touch her. But I kept my hands to myself.

"Yeah. Just shocked, that's all. You?" Gina took a step my way, but her sister blocked her path and narrowed her dark eyes on me.

"How do you know my sister?" She folded her arms in a protected stance. "It's not like you knew her before this event."

"Actually, I did—do know your sister and you too, smart ash." Cyndi's eyes widened like saucers and her mouth dropped open.

"There's only one person who used to call me that, but he was a squirt of the kid," she admonished, eyeing me up and down. "There's no way this could be the same Philly from when we were kids," she said to her sister.

"Yep, this is our Philly." Gina smiled. She reached my side and wrapped a single arm around my waist. It felt good and right to have her there.

"All this time, you knew this gorgeous hunk of a man. Hi, I'm Brandy." She snickered. "Gina has been jus—"

I never saw a woman move so fast as I did with Gina. She slapped a hard hand over her friend's mouth and whispered something so low that I couldn't hear a word. Brandy finally nodded once, and Gina dropped her hand.

"Hi, I'm Sam. I'm the easy-going one." She gave me a wave. "You are pretty to look at."

With a warning look on Gina's face, the three women clamped their lips tight.

Gina turned to me and pasted on a serene smile. "We're starving and since we won't be going anywhere anytime soon, do you want to join us for dinner?"

The touch on my arm she bestowed upon me made my heart race. "I would love to, but I have to warn you. Barb told the cops you were there. They want to talk to you about Rodney's death."

"Christ on a cracker," Sam crowed out. "Gina, what did you get yourself into?"

"Nothing," Gina countered with a frown. "I walked out

of the bathroom and found Barb screaming at the top of her lungs. I saw what she was screaming at, and I reacted too."

"Was that all, Ms. DiCaprio? Is that your real last name?" All five of us turned in the same direction to see the jerk detective hovering a few feet away. "I need you to come with me. I have many questions."

"Does she require a lawyer?" Brandy asked, stepping up like she could barricade the cop from getting closer to her friend.

"Does she have something to hide?" There was a beat of silence before his eyes swiveled to Gina. "Do you?"

Gina stepped around her friend with her chin lifted high, exuding confidence. "I don't have anything to hide."

Jesus. This woman was giving me butterflies. Actual butterflies. No woman had ever affected me the way Gina DiCaprio did back then and now. I thought reconnecting with her was the highlight of the day. But seeing her strong and confident, my feelings for her when I was a kid paled compared to what I feel now. When she looked at me for reassurance, my need to protect her rose fast, like a tsunami in a hurricane.

I would never have thought I'd be standing here, my hand out to her, and feel the way I did for my high school crush. But one thing was for damn sure... I'd lost her once, I wasn't going to let that happen again.

Chapter 3

Gina

As Gina followed the detective, the Boba Book Babes trailed two steps behind them. He stared ahead, eyes fixed on the door.

"This is such bull-crap," Sam muttered, dragging her feet.

"Gina wouldn't hurt a fly," Brandy said. "But they don't know that."

"Unless they burned books," Cyndi added. "Gina's panties would be in a bunch then."

"That's true." Brandy agreed.

"Who wouldn't?" Sam said.

The detective wheeled around, glaring at the women. "I don't understand why you're joking at a time like this. A man has been brutally murdered, and your friend is a suspect."

Blood whooshed in Gina's ears from the detective's comment, making it hard for her to breathe.

At the entrance to a small conference room turned interrogation cell, the detective opened the door and pointed for Gina to enter. She gulped and glanced over her shoulder, noticing for the first time Austin was beside her.

His warm hand landed on her shoulder and squeezed gently. "Everything will be alright." Austin's full lips tipped in a reassuring smile, which eased her worry.

"Thanks," she nodded, resisting the urge to fall into his arms.

"Austin?" a woman's voice called. "Sorry to interrupt, but I'm glad I found you. Redd and Chad are signing books while everyone is waiting to be interviewed. We need you, too." The plump volunteer smiled, but it didn't reach her eyes.

"You mean Tammy isn't shutting down the event?" Austin asked.

The woman shrugged. "Go ask her." She spun on her heel and stomped off.

"I can't believe this," he hissed.

"You go. We'll catch up with you later." Gina bit her lip.

"Are you sure?" he asked, his amber eyes scanning her.

"I've got the Boba Book Babes." Gina nodded as Brandy slung an arm over her shoulder.

"Okay. I'll see you in a bit." He hesitated just a moment, then turned, followed after the woman.

Gina rubbed her stomach and inhaled. With every step that separated them further, heaviness descended. Her friends had been talking, but she'd missed the bulk of the conversation.

"That ash would mesmerize me too," Sam smirked. Cyndi nudged her in the ribs.

"If you're done ogling the model, come inside, Miss DiCaprio." The detective's dark eyes narrowed on Gina, and he swept his arm in a grand gesture.

Gina skirted around his protruding belly into the small, frigid room. The AC droned, blowing her hair out of place and making her nipples hard enough to cut glass. She hugged herself.

Perhaps they freeze a confession out of the suspects?

The detective stepped into the room and the door closed behind him. Cyndi stuck her foot out as the door was going to latch.

His eyes zeroed in on her. "What do you want?" He barked in her face.

Cyndi wedged herself in the doorway. "This door remains open, or I get to sit with my sister."

The detective stretched, cracking his neck. "This is official police business, and I don't want a nosey interloper interrupting my investigation."

Cyndi's gaze honed in on the irritating man. She straightened her shoulders and leaned in. Gina's eyes widened, recognizing Cyndi's nobody-messes-with-my-sister-except-me expression.

"Listen here, Detective Dick, Gina volunteered to go with you. She didn't have to agree to anything unless you're charging her with something." Cyndi jabbed a finger at the detective. With each poke in the air, Gina imagined little invisible bolts of electricity zapping the rude man.

The detective's brows dipped, forming a thick V. He straightened, puffing out his chest. This peacock strut wouldn't impress or intimidate Cyndi. In fact, it'd rile her up.

Gina leaned back to watch the show.

"No, you listen—"

"I am not leaving my sister alone with a man, even if he is a so-called detective. If you want to ask her questions, fine, but you'll have to deal with me being here, too."

Cyndi's petite frame pulsated with authority. "And I want to see your badge."

The detective's jaw tightened, then his mustache twitched.

Western music played in Gina's mind. *Who'll draw first?*

Her stubborn twin, once again blocking an entry, or the gruff, impatient cop, who had the means to detain them forever. Maybe not forever, but the room was freezing, and minutes felt like hours.

With a grunt, the cop stepped back from the door. "Fine–but you have to remain quiet or I'll haul you off to jail for interfering in a murder investigation."

Sam and Brandy pushed into the room too.

"Golly, it's colder than a witch's teat in here." Sam rubbed her hands together.

Detective Burns growled, "You guys aren't supposed to be in here."

"I think we'll need some coffee to stave off the frostbite. How do you take your coffee, Detective?" Brandy asked with a cocked brow.

"Black." He grumbled, rolling his eyes. "Thanks."

Cyndi stood behind Gina, her body producing an adrenaline-induced heatwave. She patted Gina's shoulder. "You got this."

"You know how we take our coffee," Gina said with a smile.

"Sweet and creamy, like your men," Sam laughed.

"I'll help you, Sam." Rubbing her arms, Brandy trailed her out of the room.

Gina and Cyndi chuckled. "I wish I'd brought my spirit animal mug," Cyndi lamented.

The detective looked at the Babes like they were crazy

before he took a seat. He lifted a leather bi-fold, displaying his badge. Setting the ID aside, he opened a notepad to a blank page and began writing. He glanced up, pen posed. "Is DiCaprio your real last name?"

"Yes," Gina and Cyndi replied in unison.

He narrowed his eyes at Cyndi. "It seems someone thinks you're lying about being the actor's cousin."

"We do have a cousin, Leonard DiCaprio," Gina insisted.

"So, he's not the famous one, but he is an actor," Cyndi added.

"For his high school musical. He can sing, too." Gina shrugged. "When people hear our last name, they always ask if we are related to Leo. We say yes. It's a truth—"

"And a lie—" Cyndi interrupted.

"At the same time," they finished together.

Detective Burns tapped the desk with the pen. "Let me see your license?"

Gina fished inside her bag for her ID, then slid it over to the detective. "See?"

"What's your name?" He pointed to Cyndi. "And your friends' names, too."

The detective scribbled the information, then set the license aside. He tapped his pen on the paper. "Why did you come to this Pandemonium event?"

Cyndi pulled out the chair next to Gina. "This will take a few minutes." She plopped into it in time to receive an elbow in the ribs. "Hey."

"My friends, sister and I meet up at a few book events every year. It's one way we keep in touch." Gina stuck her tongue out at her sister, who rolled her eyes.

"Will you two grow up and get serious? Are you staying at the hotel?"

They nodded. "We already checked in."

"Any reason for coming to this particular event?" His dark eyes swung between the women.

"I wasn't too fond of traveling to Peoria until Cyndi mentioned Rodney Stiff as the keynote speaker and sponsor." Gina thought back to that fateful day she'd first met Rodney. Her first book signing had been his as well.

"Are you obsessed with the deceased?"

"Have you ever read his books?" Cyndi countered.

"No."

"Sure, he's easy on the eyes, but his words can carry you away. He is... or he was a phenomenal writer." Sadness engulfed Gina, and she bowed her head.

Burns leaned in, eyes sharp on her face. "How did you end up over the body?"

Gina clenched her hands together. "I wasn't over his body. I was standing next to Barb when I saw him."

"Ms. DiCaprio, tell me exactly what happened."

"They announced the event would start soon, so I hurried to the bathroom. Rodney was coming out of the men's room and almost ran into me. He was on the phone texting."

"Did you hear a name or see what he typed? Or anyone else around you during that time?"

"No. But he was angry and uttered 'that little bitch.'" Gina tried to swallow her anxiety as he continued jotting down on his notepad. "There were at least two women in the bathroom after entering the stall. They hated Rodney, and one said she was going to kill him."

"She what?" Cyndi gasped, gripping her shoulder.

"Who were they?" Detective Burns insisted.

"I never saw their faces, but one sounded as if she had a cold." Gina drummed her hands on the table. "Oh. One had white Mary Janes and had a blue teardrop tattoo on her ankle."

"What are Mary Janes?" The detective scribbled furiously without looking up.

Cyndi snickered. "They're shoes for women."

Burns glowered at Cyndi, rubbing the back of his reddened neck.

Gina passed him her phone with a picture of the shoes. "Here, Detective. This is what I'm talking about."

He glanced at it. "Can you text me that image?" He rambled out his number, and Gina quickly sent it off.

"Are we done?" Cyndi pushed.

"No. Keep explaining," he said to Gina, ignoring Cyndi..

"The ladies were gone when I exited the stall. When I left the bathroom, I was alone in the hallway." Gina inhaled. "Then I heard the scream." She hugged herself and shivered.

"We all heard it." Cyndi leaned close, putting an arm around Gina's shoulders. "It's so freaking freezing in here. I'm going to fart ice cubes."

Sam returned with a drink holder filled with four paper cups. Steam escaped the small lid holes. She passed each person a cup. "Here you go. Hot, fresh coffee."

Gina held her cup, letting the warmth permeate her frozen digits. "You are a goddess," she murmured to Sam, and then breathed in the heady aroma.

"Where's Brandy?" Cyndi asked.

Sam winked, then sipped her drink. "Mmm. That's better. Brandy took the cartful of books to the room. She said she'll meet us later. She needs to drop the kids at the pool." Gina and Cyndi groaned at the same time.

Cyndi glanced at her watch. "That will be about an hour."

"Continue," Detective Burns growled with frustration, ignoring her comment.

Gina sighed. "There was a scream, and I ran toward the sound. I thought someone needed help. I saw Barb standing there, looking down and screeching her head off. The banquet table blocked the body until I moved closer." Gina studied at the tabletop. "He stared blankly..."

"I know I asked you this, but did you notice anyone else? Other than the women in the bathroom? Maybe someone followed you into the room?"

Gina blinked. "No. I didn't see anyone until the other lady came in. The one who called 911."

"Anyone acting suspicious?" Burns asked.

"Besides the ladies who wanted him dead? No. Why don't you ask Barb? She was there first."

"Barb Fields? We already have her statement. No, Ms. DiCaprio, before you went to the bathroom." He exhaled loudly.

Gina glanced toward Sam and Cyndi. "Nothing caught my eye. Sam and I went to meet the models. Everyone seemed to be having a good time."

"Well, except for that author, remember?" Cyndi recalled. Sam and Gina nodded.

"So, the other Ms. DiCaprio, you saw this before you went to see the models?"

"No, well, yes. I didn't go see the men. I went to see Rodney—"

"We all saw the disturbance," Sam interrupted. "Gina and I went to see the cover models, and Brandy and Cyndi headed to see that dead author. A woman talked to Barb.

The little wisp of a girl was flailing her arms about like an angry Muppet trying to fly."

Cyndi nodded, covering her mouth to hide a grin. "The angry woman pointed in Rodney's direction. Then, after she stomped away, Barb turned and glared at Rodney."

"Did you hear what they said?" Detective Burns scratched something on the notepad and then took a sip of his coffee.

"No. They were too far away," Gina said, and the others nodded in agreement.

"Do you know the author?"

"Deidra Raines," Gina whispered.

Detective Burns' eyebrows rose, then he hastily jotted down her name. "What about you, Ms. DiCaprio?" He pointed his pen at Cyndi. "Why did you go see the dead author?"

Cyndi's jaw dropped, but Sam answered. "He wasn't dead then."

"I wanted a fangirl moment," Cyndi admitted, her cheeks turning rosy. "Brandy and I had our pictures taken with him." She shrugged.

"You did? Let me see it," Gina implored.

Cyndi opened her camera app. She pushed the phone toward her sister. Rodney Stiff stood between Cyndi and Brandy as the girls gazed adoringly at the author.

"Cheesy but nice," Gina teased, then frowned. "Poor Rodney." She set the phone on the table.

The detective pulled the phone to him to get a better look. He tapped the screen, enlarging the photo. After a moment, he made a note of the time.

"Detective Burns," Officer Anita Cox appeared at the door. Her hand clamped on a well-dressed man's elbow. "You've got to hear what Rodney Stiff's personal assistant has to say. His name is Harrison Busch." She pointed inside until the slender man obliged and stepped into the room.

Wearing a sneer and his nose slightly tipped up, Harrison surveyed the occupants. "Which one of you is the po-po?"

The detective stood, inflating his chest again. Harrison's sneer faltered. His gaze dropped to his manicured fingers.

"Are we done?" Gina rose from her chair while clutching the coffee cup.

Burns handed the driver's license back to Gina and the phone to Cyndi. "For now. Please don't leave the premises, ladies." Burns gave Gina his card. "We might need to speak to you again."

Gina, Cyndi, and Sam started toward the door when Harrison glanced at them with an inquisitive look before declaring, "I have a laundry list of possible suspects–all of them catty tarts."

The women skirted the man as he took a seat. As they filtered out, Gina glanced back.

Rodney's PA leaned over the table. The sneer had returned. "I know who despised my boss, and I'm almost sure they killed him."

Chapter 4

Austin

The idea of Gina dealing with that cop unnerved me. But she said she could handle it, and I believed her. Gina was as strong as back when I first met her as my neighbor.

For the first time in my young life, my mother's decision to marry my ex-step-father, Douglas Dooley, had been a good one. Trust me, I loved my mother, but she had made some horrible choices in men. I was one of those results, but she loved me unconditionally, and she proved it in ways I never wanted to mention.

Gina was my first crush. And when my mother had enough of Doug's crap, she packed our things and left.

By the time I had found out, Mom gave me a day to say goodbye. But leaving the girl who stole my heart was the hardest thing I had ever done.

I shook off those dour days and tried to focus on the idea of Gina and that hug she gave me. Now, it would be difficult to keep my head on the job I came here to do, when all I wanted to was to be with her.

I met up with the popular Scottish cover model, Redd Herrington. The hulk of a man was on a lot of historical romance covers. Next to him stood Chad Cummings. Tall and muscular, built like a runner, Chad was popular on mostly male/male romance covers.

Lately, those two had been chumming around, which was strange since they used to dislike each other.

"Is it true Rod's dead?" Redd asked as he signed a book he had posed for. "I won't believe it until I see it."

"It's probably bullshit. Did you notice the reporter outside?" Chad asked, handing out a dick sucker. "He's done this promo crap before."

"No, you idiots. Rod Stiff is dead," I scolded in a whisper. The last thing I wanted was to snag anyone's attention.

"Maybe he deserved it." Chad grabbed my biceps. "I heard he was a real asshole."

"I never had to deal with him personally. But from a few other male models that posed for his earlier covers, the author was a giant prick." Redd flicked a look at me. "Was he that way with you?"

"I dealt with his hyper-inflated ego once." I stuck up a finger.

"You're lucky then," Redd whispered when two female fans raced up and flung white T-shirts and markers out for the three of us to sign.

I pasted on a fake smile and tried to attempt to enjoy myself. I signed my name and passed the shirt to my friends. One girl handed me Rodney Stiff's book with me on the cover.

"Please, can you sign it to Tawny with a Y?" she giggled. She literally batted her fake eyelashes at me.

The other woman shoved her book in my hand and gleefully said, "Make mine out to my lover Mandy, always yours, Austin. And Mandy is also with a Y." The woman winked at me. I wanted to gag. Instead, I smiled wider and wrote what she wanted.

Why do women assume being forward is attractive? I liked boldness but not in-your-face I-want-to-do-you-right-here attitude. Believe it or not, it was off-putting to us models.

Granted, I wouldn't mind if Gina was forward... in private. The idea of having Gina alone sent a surge of excitement straight to my—

"Austin, I need you to stop daydreaming and start handing out more of these suckers. I want them all gone." Molly Caudill, Deidra Raines' PA, scowled and shoved the small basket of sweet licks into my chest. She balled her shaking hands. "And you two need to pass the rest of these postcards and bookmarks for Deidra's latest release." The bossy brunette then stalked away without looking back.

"What a bitch." One of the women standing before us said with an equal amount of haughtiness.

"How rude," her friend replied with a deep frown.

"Much apologies, ladies, for that interruption. Here, have a sucker." Redd grabbed two dicks out of the small basket and passed them one. "Now, what else can we do for you?"

"Pictures," they both screeched.

I took a step back as Redd and Chad switched positions, snapping photos with the fans' cell phones. As I watched my friends, a conversation to the left of me caught my attention.

"It's a shame he's dead. Love his books, but..."

"Me too, but doubling the price isn't worth buying any. What is he thinking?"

"I know. Now that Stiff is dead, his PA thinks the books

are worth more. I love the man's novels, but he's no Stephen King."

I turned in the direction of the irate conversation as the two women walked away from Rodney Stiff's table. Curious about what they were saying, I passed the basket to Chad. "Hold this."

As I got closer to the table, I spotted a sign that read: *Be right back.*

Under the books, there was a partially exposed piece of paper. I slid it out and glanced down with shock. It was the list of Rodney's novels and merchandise for sale. Everything on the list had been doubled. From ten dollars for each book, it went to twenty. And forget about the shirts, mugs, and other accessories that were being sold.

Looking around, I made sure no one was paying attention to me, and quickly folded the paper and tucked it into the back pocket of my jeans. I was sure the cops would love to see this.

I was about to return to where Redd and Chad were signing more swag when I overheard two PAs at the next table talking about Rodney and how the cops deemed his death a murder.

"No one is allowed to leave the hotel until everyone talks with the detective—which, by the way, is a total douche."

"I know. But I'm curious to find out who killed Rodney."

"I'm sure there's a long list of people." The woman scrunched her nose in disgust.

"I know who's on top of that list." Then both PAs turned in the direction of Deidra Raines, who was giving two other authors a what-for. The conversation between the three was heated.

"I heard the cops are speaking to Rodney's PA now." One of the PAs pointed to the table I was standing next to. They gave me a funny look before turning to each other and chuckling.

Crap, I needed to find Gina. If Harrison Busch was talking to the detective, then Gina had to be free and clear.

I headed to the other side of the huge ballroom and out through a set of closed double doors. There, seated on a group of couches, were Gina, her sister, and their friends. They were in deep discussion, and like on cue, all four women turned their heads to me.

The wide smile on Gina's face settled and warmed my chest. I didn't hesitate when I reached her side and drew her into a hug. "Are you okay?"

"Yeah. Are you?" she finally said when I pulled back and stared into her blue eyes filled with surprise.

"I'm good." I glanced down at the empty plastic cup. "Where's my boba tea?"

"Sorry, I wasn't thinking about you at the time," Brandy chirped. She raised her cup and swirled the tapioca balls in her drink. "Next time."

"Sure," I said, but my attention was back on Gina, who didn't move from my side. "I can't stay long, but I wanted to come find you and make sure you're alright."

"She's all good," Cyndi offered with a wink. "So, you can let my sister go now."

"Mind your business." Gina glared at her, then looked at me with a smile. "Don't listen to my sister. She's just jealous."

"I am not." She abruptly stood and was about to stalk off when Officer Anita Cox walked up.

"Officer Cox," Brandy quickly said. "What can we do for you?"

She glanced at Gina's friend for a fraction too long before turning her eyes on me. "Detective Burns and I would like a word with you, Mr. Blackmoor."

"Why?" Gina blurted out, her hand latched onto mine, like we're in solidarity. I liked that. For the first time in a very long while, I had someone supporting me.

"Mr. Blackmoor, can you come with me, please?"

"Then I'm coming with you," Gina insisted, brooking no argument.

"Just tell us, so Gina doesn't lose her mind thinking her boy toy is heading off to jail," Brandy said in a sweet tone.

I glared at Brandy because I wasn't a boy toy kind of guy... unless Gina wanted me to be. But all four women looked at Brandy with mixed emotions on their faces I couldn't decipher.

Sam, Gina, and Cyndi gawked disbelievingly at their friend, whereas the cop scowled.

There were several beats of silence before Officer Cox finally shook her head. "Fine, but you need to keep it under your belt."

They all nodded like bobbleheads.

"Promise," Gina said. She offered a small smile to me and whispered, "I don't see you as my boy toy, but we could have fun with that concept." She gave me a knowing wink, which shot straight to my groin.

"Stop," I muttered before my pants tented.

"Yeah, stop," Cyndi exclaimed, covering her ears.

Sam waved her hands in the air, catching our attention. "I want to know what Officer Cox has to say before she hauls Gina's man away."

Ooh, I liked hearing I'm her man.

"Sorry. Go ahead." Gina used her fingers and pretended to zip her lips.

Cox's eyes pinched in annoyance as she expelled a heavy breath. "We found out what was sticking out of Mr. Stiff's mouth. It was a phallus sucker. The coroner thinks it's the cause of the author's death, but he won't be able to determine that until he does a further investigation of the body. But we did check the stick for fingerprints and found one."

"You're not saying what I think you're saying," Gina uttered, her fingers tightened even more around mine.

"Yes, I am." Officer Cox fixed me with a scrutinizing stare. "Your name came up right away, Mr. Blackmoor. You need to come with me now. If you decide to resist, then I'll have no option but to put you under arrest, take you back to the police station, and we can talk there. It's your choice."

What choice do I have?

Chapter 5

Gina

Gina's heart rate climbed. *Why had Austin's name alerted the officer?* She studied Austin's brooding eyes, now darker in the shadow of his furrowed brow. His chiseled jaw clenched.

She squeezed his hand, calling his attention.

"Everything will be alright," she whispered. Once the words left her mouth, her mind flashed to the women in the bathroom before Rodney's death. The woman had reassured her friend the same way and look how that had turned out.

A murderer was still at large.

Gina's Philly wouldn't have harmed anyone. He loved animals to the point that when they had walked to the bus stop, he used to step over worms on the pavement.

But cute, sweet Philly had grown up into hot cover model Austin. A lot could happen in a decade.

Could a killer hide behind that handsome face?

Austin's gaze rose and met hers. She searched it for

hints of something... He scanned her, and her breath caught. His brows lifted, and his shoulders slowly drooped.

What did he see on my face?

Gina opened her mouth to reassure him.

"Come on, Mr. Blackmoor, while I'm still young." Officer Cox motioned over her shoulder.

Austin sighed and stepped forward. Cox about-faced with her hands on her utility belt.

Gina glanced at her friends. Sam wrung her hands. Brandy chewed her lip while her gaze fixated on the police-woman's handcuffs. Gina met Cyndi's eyes.

"Breathe," Cyndi reminded Gina.

Gina inhaled deeply and nodded to her twin. She squared her shoulders. "Wait."

Austin jerked to a stop, his lips tipped in a hopeful, cockeyed smile. She hurried to his side, touching his arm. He turned to face her fully.

She'd wanted to reassure him and offer encouragement, but her entire life's worth of words failed her. Her face heated under his tender gaze, then her eyes dropped to his lips. Burning ignited deep in her soul. She fisted his shirt, pulling him closer. On her tiptoes, Gina claimed his lips. Her heart threatened to launch itself to the moon.

"Yeehaw," Sam hooted.

"Let's see some tongue," Brandy taunted.

Sam laughed. "You go, girl."

"Gross," Cyndi admonished.

Letting go of her hold without breaking the kiss, Gina raised her arm, then her middle finger, to her sister.

"Well, I never," Cyndi gasped in mock horror.

Gina broke the too-short, G-rated kiss, much to her body's disappointment. She grinned at Austin and whispered, "That's exactly why she's always so salty."

"Let's go," Officer Cox prompted once more.

Austin sighed, the smile falling from his face.

Gina squeezed his arm. "You've got this." He nodded, meeting her eyes. "When you're done, come find me." She winked and released him.

He walked away, and her heart hitched. How could so little time together stir up all the feelings she thought she'd put to rest?

Austin was innocent, and so was Gina. She spun, rubbing her hands. "Listen, ladies. There's a killer on the loose. We need to find them, and we've got to figure out how Rodney Stiff became..."

"A stiff?" Brandy volunteered.

"I agree. That detective doesn't know shit from Shinola," Cyndi said, folding her arms.

"Where should we start?" Brandy asked, gazing in the direction the officer and Austin had gone.

"Who was the first to find him?" Gina pursed her lips together, not wanting to blurt who she thought was the most obvious suspect.

"Barb," Sam, Brandy, and Cyndi said in unison. Their heads all swiveled toward the ballroom containing the book signing.

"Let's go," Cyndi announced, leading the pack.

Gina fell in line behind her sister. Now that she had a mission to focus her thoughts, her hands stopped shaking.

Clumps of people gathered near various tables inside the room. The scene seemed familiar, yet somber. Eight-foot tables with black tablecloths lined the parameter. Tables also formed rows, creating traffic flow for the readers to follow.

Vibrant banners accented each table, announcing the author's name, social media, and a book cover or two. Books in piles or on small shelves were arranged on the tabletops along with swag, like pens and stickers.

"Oh, man. There's awesome swag at this event," Brandy said, picking up a metal bookmark with a handcuff charm dangling off the end.

Sam ignored Brandy's comment and scanned the aisle. She pointed toward the far side. "Isn't that Barb?"

"Where?" Cyndi asked, struggling to see over the throng of people milling about.

"Sitting at the information table," Sam replied, pointing toward the far end of the long room.

The crowd parted momentarily, and Gina caught a glimpse of a woman bowed over with her face in her hands. Her shoulders shook. When she glanced up with a pallid, tear-stained face, she took an offered tissue. A swarm of volunteers in royal blue shirts buzzed around, protecting the upset woman.

"Can I have your attention, please?" Tammy, the event coordinator, stood on a chair with a mic, waving her free arm. The room hushed, and the readers turned to face her. "Hey everyone. In light of what happened to our keynote speaker and sponsor, we will continue with the Pandemonium in Peoria event in his honor. Please visit the conference rooms with the raffle baskets and other items up for auction. Tickets are available for purchase. If anyone has any knowledge regarding the accident, please come to the information table. Thank you."

A bunch of ladies with bourbon-colored shirts blocked Gina's view. A gray-haired older lady strode toward the Boba Book Babes with her nose in the air. The woman glanced over at the Book Babes long enough to read one of their shirts and watch Sam suck a boba up the straw. The snooty leader rolled her eyes and continued strolling by.

Beside her, a shorter young man with guyliner and earrings struggled to match her gait. The back of her shirt read: Boozy Book Bitches.

"What's up her butt?" Brandy asked with her hands on her hips.

"She's a blogger. It's not a very good one either," Gina responded. She glanced at Cyndi, then burst out laughing.

Cyndi had contorted her face as if she smelled a big steaming pile of dooty. And her eyes... it appeared she'd tried to roll her crossed eyes.

Like sheep, four other women followed the stuck-up leader.

"I don't think we can talk with Barb right now," Brandy lamented. "Not privately anyway."

"She's still upset," Sam added.

"Or she's a great actress," Cyndi mentioned with a shrug.

Gina turned to witness Harrison Busch slip behind Rodney's author table. The leader of the Boozy Book Bitches stood with her hands on her hips. She waved her arms and shouted Harrison's name, but he ignored her.

"What do you think, Gina?" Cyndi indicated with her head. "Talk to the PA before Barb?"

"Ooo. He's making that lady with a stick up her butt mad." Sam grinned. "I want to go watch."

"Fine. But keep your eyes open for creepy vibes or sketchy people." Gina said.

"Another one of you voodoo-woodoo feelings again." Brandy wiggled her fingers in Gina's face.

"Stop." Cyndi shooed Brandy away from her twin. "Those feelings have served us well over the years."

Gina walked to Penny Buttons' table next to Rodney's. Sam stayed beside Gina while Brandy and

Cyndi meandered to Keeley Wetstone's table on the far side of Rod's.

Harrison propped up a framed list of books with a black line through the prices.

Gina picked up a paperback with a ripped man in a kilt. "Taking the Highlander by the Hilt." The double entendre had Gina giggling. She flipped it over and pretended to read the blurb while listening to the Boozy Bitch get huffy.

"Why are you charging more? I don't understand," the snobby one growled.

"Because he's dead." Harrison barely glanced up as he shuffled things in a box. He set the box aside and lifted the tablecloth, pulling out a new container. "Where is it?" he mumbled. He turned, tapping his chin.

"This is ridiculous," the Boozy boy sidekick groused.

"If you don't like it, then move along." Harrison waved them off with a frown.

Gina set the highlander book down and glanced over at Rodney's banner. His likeness stared at her, pleading, *Find my killer*. She gulped. Even if he was a royal douchebag, he didn't deserve death by penis pop.

Slam!

Gina and Sam jumped. The Boozy Book Bitch slapped her hand on the tabletop, toppling the neat piles of books. A smarmy smile had claimed her lips. "I demand you sell the books at the pre-order price."

Harrison turned crimson as he stopped searching the inventory. His spine straightened, and his brows pinched in conjunction with his frown.

"I don't think so, Jacki. Especially after the shitty review you wrote about *Saving the Dragon Daddy*. It's a wonder the police aren't after you."

"Cherry wrote that review, but I agree with her. It's a ridiculous plot. The characters aren't believable. Rod really disappointed us this time around." Jacki rapped the table with her knuckles. "But I still want it for my library. How about a deal?"

"Now see here, honey. It is what it is, and if you won't buy it for the new price, then I suggest you go to therapy and get over it." Harrison glared at each of the Boozy crew in turn. One eyebrow twitched when he noticed the man.

"I paid ten for a pre-order, and I want another book for ten." The Boozy boy tried batting his lashes.

Harrison shook his head. "Mmm... No." He crossed his arms.

"It's okay, Ricky," Jacki cooed, patting his arm. "Harry Busch can't give you what you need."

The group cackled, then they all stomped away.

"What a shrew." Harrison snarled, glaring daggers at Jacki's back. He returned his attention to the inventory, frantically shifting items. "Where's the damn laptop? He's going to be mad."

Gina met Sam's eyes. They shared a questioning expression. Who is *he*?

Chapter 6

Austin

"You know this is a bunch of crap. I'm not the only one who touched those suckers." I glared at Officer Cox. She kept her cool gaze averted and stayed completely silent. I shook my head. I should, too, since my mouth tended to run away from me when I was angry.

As we approached the door where the detective was standing, Molly, Deidra Raines' personal assistant, scrambled out of the room with her eyes cast toward the floor.

"Have a seat, Mr. Blackmoor." Detective Burns pointed to the chair adjacent to a four-foot-long table in the center of the room.

I took the seat he offered and kept my mouth shut until the questions commenced.

Burns sat and started glancing through some papers in a folder. I didn't know what he was looking at, or if it pertained to me. But his intimidation tactic made me nervous. Frustration also coursed through my veins, sitting here away from Gina. I wanted more time to reacquaint myself with my old crush.

"Are you going to just sit there and read, or are you going to ask me questions?" I declared as I studied the man. Middle-aged—maybe in his late forties. Probably nearing the five-ten mark in height and had a protruding gut that showed he liked to eat.

He closed the folder, slapped it down, and leaned in. Hard eyes on me. He began his questioning. "So, you're a cover model."

I wasn't expecting that. "Last time I checked."

Burns huffed. "Funny. I didn't know you could make money showing off your body on books. Maybe I should try it. I need a few extra bucks in my account."

"I can give you my agent's number. Can I leave now?"

"Mr. Blackmoor." He blew out a breath, which stank of old coffee and something else. "We can do the questioning here or back at the station. It's your choice." A tick appeared on the man's jaw. It was proof that he wasn't messing with me.

"Yes. I'm a cover model. It doesn't pay the bills—if that's what you're asking." I wasn't about to tell the man he would starve if he got into the business. Looking at his gut, he could shed a few pounds. But I digressed. "Modeling is a part-time gig for me. I'm a full-time carpenter," I said evenly, keeping my face neutral.

"Where?"

I winced when he asked because the name of Bartholomew's company was so far left field, and I'm slightly embarrassed to say. However, the smirk on the cop's face proved that he knew where I worked.

So, I told him. "Blu Ballers Construction." The man's lips twitched slightly. On the other hand, I couldn't keep the stoic demeanor any longer and busted out laughing. "Sorry."

Burns cleared his throat, lost his smile, and asked the next question. "Where were you during the time of the incident? And please explain to me how your fingerprints got on the stick."

"I was passing out the suckers and swag alongside the other cover models. Redd Herrington and Chad Cummings. They can vouch for me," I explained. "We were in the main banquet hall greeting the fans. Anyone could have had access to those penis suckers. Whoever killed Rodney happened to grab one with my prints on it," I declared with my arms across my chest.

"We'll be the judge of that. Now, can you tell me the time when this happened?" Burns asked as he reopened the folder, and I got to see what was inside.

My life was on those papers. My mom, the numerous step-dads' names, where I worked, and the bit of trouble I was in when I hit seventeen and hung out with the wrong crowd.

"Mr. Blackmoor?"

My eyes cut to the detective, who studied me like a honed knife, sharp and pointed.

"I don't know exactly what time, but I arrived at the hotel and checked in at four. Right after I dropped my stuff in the room, I came down to look for the event coordinators."

"Did you have any issues with the victim, Mr. Blackmoor?" I hated the way he said my name. It was almost degrading.

"No."

The cop's thick-graying eyebrows rose high. "Are you sure about that?"

I didn't like his tone. It was accusatory.

"Yes. Why?" I bit back.

The man pulled out a notebook from the inside pocket of his jacket and read from it.

"I was told you had a fight with the author a month or so back. Can you explain to me what it was about?" I stiffened at his question.

Shit. I was hoping the photoshoot Rodney wanted me to participate in wouldn't be brought up. Normally, he'd send his instructions through his PA, Harrison. But for some reason, Rodney was there instead. I hated to admit it, but that asshole had tried to manipulate me into taking off all my clothes and posing nude for his next cover.

"It would shoot the book into the stratosphere and make you a star." His words, not mine, popped into my head.

"Mr. Blackmoor, do you need more time to come up with—"

"What I'm about to tell you is the truth," I growled, even more pissed off than before. Someone threw me under the bus, and from the guilty look on Molly's face when she raced out of the room, I could clearly see it had to be her. "Rodney wanted me completely naked for the shoot for his next book. I refused. We argued. I won, and that was the end of it."

"Was it a physical altercation?" Burns asked as he jotted something on the notepad.

"No. Just a verbal one." My teeth clenched tight, and I gave no more. Shifting, the paper in my back pocket crumpled. Crap. I'd forgotten Harrison Busch's price gouging. I slid the paper over to Burns. "You might be interested in this. I found it on Rodney Stiff's table. A couple of PAs were upset with Harrison about the price change."

Burns nodded, then looked at the crinkled paper and then the folder chronicling my life. "I would like you to stick around the hotel. I might have more questions for you."

"Fine. I'm not going anywhere since the event is still on," I uttered while I glanced at the door that swung open, and Officer Cox strode in.

"I have Deidra Raines outside," she said, but stared at me with a look I couldn't decipher.

"That's my cue." I walked out of the room as the author bitched her way inside.

I ignored her rancorous glare and went to look for Gina. As I rounded the corner to the hotel entryway, I was stopped by Tammy Shaver. She ogled me like I was her main course. I shivered at the idea of this woman touching me again. It's not because she was ugly—no, she was a mean, spiteful woman, because I wouldn't sleep with her. She tried to bar me from this event, but Rodney insisted I'd come.

"Can I have a word with you, Austin?" Tammy purred. She hitched her lips up in invitation, and her two-inch long talons called nails clacked together when she waved me over. Like that was going to get me cowed into doing her nasty bidding. No way. Especially now that I had Gina.

She was someone special. The woman in front of me could go jump in the river across the street for all I cared.

"Sure, what?" I kept some space between us and folded my arms across my chest, which cut off her access to touch my pecs.

"Come and have a drink with me at the hotel bar. What did the detective ask you? I want to be prepared when the cops talk to me again."

Are you shitting me?

"I can't talk about it. Besides, I have plans with Redd and Chad. See ya, Tammy." At that moment, my two friends walked out of the banquet room. I rushed to their side and told them under my breath to keep moving.

"Why are we walking this way?" Redd asked, chuckling.

"Dragon Lady at six o'clock," I said quietly so no one but them could hear me.

"She grabbed my ass when I checked in. Who frickin' does that?" Chad rumbled out.

"She does," Redd and I said at the same time.

"She wants me to join her for drinks at the bar. I told her no, but I'm meeting an old acquaintance and her girl-friends there."

"I can't believe Tammy's trying that again. Doesn't she know none of us like her?"

"Apparently not, if she keeps asking," Chad chuckled.

"Want to join me and the girls?" I asked them.

"Sorry, I have to Facetime my mom at eight. Raincheck?" Redd asked as he took out his cell. His mother was a manipulative woman. And a jealous one at that. But Redd loved her and worshiped the ground she walked on. Once a mama's boy, always a mama's boy.

"Fine." I turn to my other friend. "Chad?"

"Sure. For a few minutes. I have plans later, but I'm sure one drink won't hurt," he smiled.

I liked Chad. We hit it off right from the start. He's a great cover model and has been on quite a few covers since he started two years ago.

We left Redd in the lounge area with his call and headed to the bar. As I stepped inside, I spotted Gina and the girls right away. She was waving her hands at me to come.

"I'm heading to the bar to order a drink," Chad called to me. "What do you want?"

"Get me a Gray Goose and Seven-Up," I said, not paying any attention to where I was walking and accidentally bumped into someone. "Sorr—" The word died in my throat.

Standing in front of me, a hand on my right pec, was Tammy. "I thought you had plans with the boys?" she asked as she slid the same hand to my stomach.

Backing away, I made sure I wasn't giving out mixed signals. "I did, and now I'm here to see my *girlfriend*." I thumbed in the direction where Gina was sitting.

"No, you're not. You came to see me," Tammy gushed as she stepped toward me.

Big mistake. The second she took another step, Gina appeared next to me and wrapped her arms around my waist. "Hey, baby." The words came out sweet, but the look of fire in her eyes had me smiling huge.

Brandy, Cyndi, and Sam were right behind us, waving.

"Tammy, I want you to meet my girlfriend, Gina DiCaprio."

"So, you're the DiCaprio? Like the movie star, huh?" Tammy had disgust written across her face.

"Leo's my cousin," Gina countered smoothly. "Now, if you excuse me, I'm going to take my man and feed him."

Anger fused Tammy's cheeks even more when Gina leaned onto her tippy toes and kissed my lips. It was brief but wonderful. I squeezed her tighter to me and walked off. "See you, Tammy." Gina smiled over her shoulder.

"Yeah, see ya," Brandy added, sauntering past Tammy.

Gina slipped into the bench first. I sat next to her. In the center of the table was a big, round plate of nachos with all the fixings, a pile of wings, and loaded potato skins.

"Now, what were we talking about before Gina almost

had a smackdown with the man stealer?" Cyndi chuckled as she grabbed some wings and a few potato skins.

"We were talking about what Harrison said earlier. I want to know whose laptop he was looking for. His or Rodney's?" Sam threw out with suspicion. She took a long sip of whatever fruity concoction she was drinking and then added, "I bet he's trying to steal Rodney's unpublished stories."

"Always the conspiracist. What I want to know is who is going to be angry?" Brandy asked while heaping a pile of nachos and cheese onto her plate.

"What laptop and who's angry?" I asked, staring at the food.

"Eat, Philly," Gina insisted and passed a plate to me. "Sorry. Austin."

"No worries. And thank you for thinking of me," I uttered. She winked, and I dug in. "So, what are you talking about?"

"We saw Harrison looking for a laptop when he got into a verbal scuffle with the Boozy Book Bitch bloggers," Gina explained between small bites of the potato skins.

"He was saying that someone a *he* was going to be mad. And we're trying to figure out who *he* is," Brandy added with a crunch.

Between the food and talking with the girls, I realized Chad hadn't brought my drink over.

Where is he? I glanced at my watch. Then I caught sight of my friend with Harrison, out of all people. Their hands were linked as they rushed out of the bar as though someone chased them with a knife.

Or maybe a dick sucker?

Chapter 7

Gina

The red numbers increased as the elevator ascended to the fifth floor. Gina couldn't wait to get to her room. All she wanted was to open a bottle of wine, throw on sweats, kick back and relax. The elevator paused long enough for Gina to wonder if something had gone wrong. She leaned against Austin's hard body for comfort. Brandy met her gaze as it jolted to a stop, and the doors hissed open.

"It's been a day," Sam mumbled as she stepped into the hallway.

"That's the understatement of the century," Cyndi replied with a frown.

They turned left and walked midway down the hall. Brandy pressed her keycard to the lock, and it flashed green. She pushed the door open and stalked inside.

Gina paused outside the doorway. "Thank you for walking me to my room," she said to Austin. The door swung shut, and Austin's arm shot out to keep it from slamming.

"Anytime." He smiled, causing the butterflies in her stomach to take flight.

"Why don't you invite him in?" Sam winked as she pushed open the room door next to Gina and Brandy's.

"Remember the wine," Cyndi added and followed Sam inside. The door closed, leaving Gina and Austin alone in the hall.

Gina met his gaze and was suddenly reluctant to part company. "Do you want to come in for a bit?"

"Sure." A smile lit his face.

"Great." She led the way. The typical hotel room had two queen beds with white bedding, taupe striped tone on tone walls, and casino-themed framed art. Luckily, she and Brandy hadn't messed up the suite.

"Austin is coming in," Gina announced for Brandy's sake.

"Cool," she said, momentarily glancing up from her bed. Brandy had emptied her VIP event bag. "Yeah, I'm a swag-whore."

She'd started organizing the paper items: bookmarks, stickers, and business cards. The little organza bags were dumped, and the contents sorted. She unwrapped a chocolate kiss and popped it into her mouth.

Gina glanced at the pile of books next to the flatscreen. All of them held Austin's likeness on the cover. Luckily, the spines faced away from them, and the top novel was flipped over.

Someone knocked on the door between the dresser with the flatscreen and the round table. "Hey y'all, open up." Sam's muffled voice filtered through the wood.

Gina opened it, revealing Sam in her piggy sweatpants and an oversized shirt. "That was fast," Gina said, shaking her head.

"What can I say? Comfort is my priority." Sam giggled, then displayed a bottle of wine. "I'd say after the day we've had, mainly you, we need a tall glass of fermented grape juice."

"That sounds heavenly." Gina glanced over at Austin with a smirk.

"I'm down." Austin reached for the bottle. "Where's your corkscrew?"

"Oh, poopers! I knew there was something I forgot," Sam lamented.

"There's one in the VIP bag." Brandy lifted a small corkscrew. "Penelope Carter swag. Score." She tossed it toward Austin, and he snatched it out of the air. He set the bottle on the table and worked on uncorking it.

"Thank you, Penelope Carter," Gina said, sitting on the edge of her bed.

"Your VIP bag is on the chair." Brandy pointed to the burgundy armchair next to Austin. "Carrying all of your bags at once was heavy."

"Whatever." Cyndi appeared in the doorway, holding empty hotel glass tumblers. "You threw everything into your cart. I don't want to hear it."

Brandy shrugged her shoulders.

"Thanks for bringing them up," Gina said with a smile. "I'm glad I didn't have to carry it around all evening." She smothered a yawn with her hand.

Austin popped the cork and poured them each a glass. He handed them out, then sat next to Gina on the bed. His thigh brushed hers. Sipping the wine and touching Austin warmed Gina. She relaxed, and her shoulder rubbed his as she grinned at him.

Sam snatched her bag. "Who wants my book stuff?"

"I'll take it," Brandy said, bouncing to her feet.

"Fine. I'll trade you for your candy." With an evil grin, Sam disappeared into her room.

Brandy contemplated her pile of sugary goodness for a moment. "Well, shit." She scooped up the pile with both hands and hurried after Sam. A few pieces slipped through her fingers, tumbling to the floor. "Watch out, swag-whore coming through."

Gina glanced at the wayward sweets and froze. Austin must have felt her stiffen. "What's wrong?"

She pointed at a red penis lollipop. Rodney's face, frozen in that vacant stare, flashed in her mind. Gina squeezed her eyes shut, but the image remained.

"Come here." Cautious of her wine, Austin pulled her onto his lap. She buried her face in his neck while he rubbed her back. "It's been one helluva day, but I wouldn't trade it for anything because it brought you to me again."

She nodded, breathing in his spicy fragrance. They'd only been reacquainted for a few hours, yet it felt as if he'd never left. His familiarness comforted her.

"Remember that night?" Austin whispered in a husky tone.

Gina nodded again. "I'm glad you found the courage to come over."

"I had to let you know how I felt before leaving. And..."

She pulled away and met his gaze. "And?"

He glanced into the other room, and then returned his attention to Gina. "And... there was no harm if you rejected me."

Smirking, Gina chuckled. "Like I would have done that. I'm pretty sure I crushed on you harder than you did on me." She drank her last sip of wine.

"I doubt it," Austin said, then finished his as well. Gina took their glasses and set them on the table. She peered into the other room where her friends and sister had spread out their VIP loot, comparing and negotiating for trade.

Gina stooped and picked up an individually wrapped breath mint, Reese's cup, and the phallus sucker from the floor. She dropped them on Brandy's bed. "Odd how a silly candy could cause so much chaos and death." She shivered.

Austin jumped up and spun her into his arms. "What do you say we get out of here?" Cocooned in his warmth, she didn't want to move.

"Get a room," Cyndi teased with a wink.

Gina sighed, rubbing her forehead. She was half-tempted to throw the dick sucker at her sister, but with her luck, it'd probably land with the stick impaling Cyndi's eye or inside her big-fat-always-open mouth. And God knows, Gina didn't want to be blamed for another murder.

"Where would we go? Back down to the bar?" Gina whispered.

A devilish grin split his lips. "I thought we could go to my room."

"Oh?" she squeaked. Several ideas about how he could make her forget the murder scrolled through her mind, all of them pleasurable.

She broke away from his embrace. "Do you have any alcohol?"

"No, but we could order—"

"It's fine. I've got another bottle in the fridge." Gina removed the wine and headed toward the door. She paused outside the closet, which was partially open. A tiny fluorescent pink feather on the floor caught her eye. "What the heck..."

"What is it?" Austin asked as she opened the closet. He stared at the feather, but Gina gazed at the clothing bar with hangers.

"Look. Fuzzy handcuffs."

"Hmm, that's something you don't find in a hotel every day."

"Actually..." Gina glanced back toward the other room, where the girls were laughing and talking. She leaned in, lowering her voice. "This is the second time I've found handcuffs in the closet at a hotel."

"You're kidding me."

"No. It's a mystery. Both times I was rooming with Brandy." Gina giggled. Brandy had insisted the first pair hadn't belonged to her, but now Gina couldn't be sure.

Austin took the bottle from Gina, and she grabbed her phone and keycard from the table.

Cyndi stuck her head into the room. Her eyes zeroed in on the hotel keycard in Gina's hand. "Where are you going?"

Resting a hand on her hip, she cocked it to the side. "We're taking your advice and getting a room," Gina declared, daring her sister to reply.

Cyndi's eyebrows shot heavenward, and her lips pulled into a smirk. Then the tease fell from her face. "But there's a killer on the loose."

"I'll protect Austin," Gina countered.

"Don't worry, Cyndi, I'll protect her with my life." Austin's face transformed into one of determination.

"Let 'em go," Sam called. "I'd rather be screwing a model, too."

"Magic dick protection," Brandy added with a laugh.

"Oh, my God," Gina groaned. She grabbed Austin by the arm and pulled him toward the exit. "Let's get out of here before I kill my friends."

They strode through the abandoned hallway. Austin

pushed the elevator's call button, and they waited, watching the arrows above the door.

"I'm sorry about the girls." Gina cast a sidelong glance at Austin. "They never miss an opportunity to tease."

"I've heard worse," he said, turning to inspect the space.

"I bet you have." Gina bit her lower lip. As a model, she imagined he'd experienced all sorts of innuendos, lude comments, and propositions.

Besides their history, why was he hanging out with her? She wasn't as glamorous or drop-dead gorgeous as other models, authors, or even some readers. But she'd caught him studying her like a lion watches a lone gazelle. And his touch had been more like a lover's caress. She trembled, her body reacting to his attention.

Does he want me for more than a one-night stand?

Austin, her childhood crush and the standard she had silently compared all her boyfriends to, had risen above the bar he'd set.

The door swished open on the other elevator. The overhead light had burned out and with the dark mahogany paneling, it seemed cave-like. Austin entered and pushed the seven button. Ambient light shone from under the railing, reflecting off the glossy tan marble.

"Spooky." Gina sidled up next to him.

"Romantic." He dropped his arm over her shoulder and tugged her close.

I could get used to this.

The door slid open. Austin took her by the hand and led her down the hallway. Muffled male voices came from the room next to Austin's.

The little green light flashed, allowing them entry to his room. A cool breeze greeted them. She rubbed her arms. "You like it chilly," she observed.

"All the better for cuddling." Austin winked and flipped on a light.

The room was similar to hers, with one glaring difference: the king-sized bed.

"Grab the glasses while I open the bottle." Austin set it on the table. He glanced up when she appeared by his side. "I forgot to bring the opener."

"It's okay." Gina handed the cups to Austin, then picked up the bottle and unscrewed the lid. "Nothing but the best." They chuckled. She poured them each a glass. "I'm glad you're sharing it with me because otherwise, I might have stuck a straw in the bottle to forget..." She glanced into the blush liquid.

Austin nudged her. "Let's toast."

Gina smiled and faced him, raising her cup. "Sure."

"To the Peoria book event bringing us back together."

"To Pandemonium in Peoria. And here's to a quiet, uneventful evening." She clinked his glass, then raised it to her lips.

"I was hoping tonight would be a little eventful, at least between you and me," he smirked.

Filled with mischief, his sultry gaze swept her body. She kept from inhaling the sip of wine and swallowed.

"What do you have in mind?" she asked, feeling a flush on her cheeks. Staring into his amber-colored eyes, they took her breath away.

"What don't I have in mind?" Austin wiggled his brows. He stepped closer.

Gina tipped her glass and gulped. She inhaled deeply, trying to calm her runaway heart. Is it possible to do more than snuggle with her book cover boyfriend? She sat on the edge of the bed and kicked off her shoes.

Austin topped off their cups, then joined her on the bed.

"I have a confession." Gina stared into her wine.

"What's that?"

"Well...," she met his gaze, and her face blushed with heat. "I've got a crush on my book boyfriend."

Austin froze mid-sip, his eyes wide. "Say that again?"

"I've been holding a torch for a hunky cover model. He's super sexy." Gina wiggled her brows.

"Me?" He pointed to himself.

"See any other cover models?"

A wicked smile spread over his full lips and made Gina tingle all over.

She cleared her throat. "How did you become a cover model?"

"It's a long story."

"We've got time tonight."

Austin rubbed his chin. "Would you like the full twelve years in detail or the abbreviated version?"

"Whatever you'd like." She patted his thigh.

"Long story short: after I moved, I fell in with a bad group and had a few scrapes with the law. Nothing serious. The wrong place and time, with the wrong sort of people. I grew up and found something I love to do and seem to have a knack for."

"What's that?" Gina pulled her legs up, sitting cross-legged. She sipped her wine, remembering the younger man's face. The troubled teen wasn't the Philly she had known.

"Woodworking. I'm a carpenter." Austin glanced at his drink. "The owner of the company I work for has a sister who's an author. She wanted a construction worker on the cover of a book and saw me. The rest is history."

There was a comfortable beat of silence where Gina pictured Austin in a hard hat, tight jeans with a tool belt slung low on his hips and shit kickers. *Mm-hmm.* She needed to find that novel.

"And what is the title of the book?"

"It was an erotic novella," he chuckled, "*Nailed Hard.*"

Gina giggled and made a mental note to order it.

"Do you work the wood with your hands?" The unfiltered question popped out of Gina's mouth.

His head shot up, and his honey gaze fixed on her. "Would you like to learn? I can show you how."

Gina's mouth watered. Heat pooled in her core. *Yes, please.* Austin leaned in, his mouth a breath away from her ear.

"What did the carpenter do after the one-night stand?" he whispered, then kissed her cheek.

"I don't know," she replied. She shivered when he kissed her collarbone.

"The second nightstand." Austin pulled back, his eyes glinting with mirth. "Get it?"

Gina groaned, shaking her head. "Carpenter humor."

"I nailed it." He chuckled.

She nudged him in the side. "You must be so proud of your shelf." It was Austin's turn to groan, then they laughed.

"How about you, Gina? What do you do for a living?"

"I'm an interior decorator. I help people make their homes pretty." She shrugged, taking a sip.

"Is it hard working with people?"

"Not usually. Sometimes they only want to be told what they picked will work, and other times I've been given free rein," Gina admitted.

"I knew you'd do it. You were always artsy." He reached out and stroked her arm.

An electric current zapped her. She glanced at his tanned, manicured hand. His warm thumb slid over her smooth skin, sending tingles up and down her spine. She squeezed her eyes shut, enjoying his nearness.

Austin shifted on the bed. "After that night, I thought of you often."

Her eyes popped open, and she frowned. "Not enough to write or call."

Austin stood, took their empty glasses and set them next to the bottle.

He combed his fingers through his hair. "I couldn't. Every time I tried, it hurt too much. I didn't know how to cope with losing you." He returned to her side.

Gina studied his lost, childlike expression. She touched his face. His five o'clock shadow tickled her fingertips. "I thought about you, too. I really missed you."

As if in slow motion, Austin lowered his head and gave her a sweet kiss. He pulled back, meeting her gaze.

"Why the hell did you stop?" She growled, fisting his shirt and jerking him close. She claimed his mouth in a clash of tongue and teeth and all twelve years of pent up longing.

His hands plunged into her long hair, holding her to him as he lowered her to the bed. Her hands delved under his shirt, skimming his tight abs.

"You don't know how long I've wanted to finish what we started that night." His warm breath fanned her cheek, as he continued to consume her lips.

She moaned under his skillful touch. His erection pressed against her, and she recalled palming the bulge through his pants all those years ago.

They flipped over, and Gina gazed at him with a sultry smile. "My dad's alarm won't interrupt us tonight," she declared. "Nothing will."

She leaned over and kissed his lips and chin, and then worked her way down his neck. He pulled off his shirt, granting her access to the most gorgeous body she'd laid eyes on. Photoshopping his torso couldn't improve perfection. She continued nipping and sucking her way down his chest.

"Your hair smells good," he murmured, bringing strands to his nose.

Gina ran a finger under his waistband, teasing the happy trail. With a finger hooked on the belt loop, she began working to remove his belt. His erection strained his jeans. Her knuckles skimmed the zipper as she undid his pants.

"To slow," he groaned.

She flashed a wicked grin and grabbed the zipper's pull tab, tugging it tooth by tooth and exposing his black boxer briefs.

"Gina, you're killing me."

"I'm savoring the moment," she whispered, meeting his hooded gaze. Nothing could deter her. Austin was hers for the night. And hopefully–

Thud. Crash.

Gina jumped to her feet, whirling around, her heart in her throat. The casino picture swayed slightly on the wall.

"What the hell?" Austin growled as he clambered out of bed.

Voices erupted from the room next door. "You threw a glass at me," someone screamed in a high-pitched tone.

"Asshole. Grow up..." The second man's voice was deeper and harder to hear.

"How dare you!" The first man screeched. "How can I walk with all this broken glass on the carpet?"

More bumping and scuffing, as if they were forcefully redecorating the room. Expletives flew with the higher voice repeatedly hollering, "Get out!"

"The notebook to the police..."

"Don't you threaten me."

"Stiff..."

"Do you know who is rooming next to you?" Concerned and quite curious, Gina leaned close to the wall to better hear the men. "Could it be a reader or author?"

Austin shook his head. "No, but I might have an idea. Let's listen from the hall and see if my guess is right."

He zipped his jeans, then headed for the door with Gina on his heels. He opened it a crack and peered out. Gina pushed in close, glimpsing a person in a hooded one-piece pajama getup who disappeared around the far corner.

The arguing had drawn other onlookers. Directly across from Austin's room, a man with a gray handlebar mustache stood with his hands in his burgundy robe pockets. His eyes narrowed on the door where the disturbance was coming from.

The yelling continued. This time, every word was unfiltered and louder through the crack under the door.

"I don't know who killed him," the high voice wailed. "Maybe you did, limp dick."

"Don't be ridiculous," the deep voice scolded.

The door next to the mustache man's room opened wide. Gina recognized two of the Boozy Book Bitches, the leader Jacki and her minion Ricky. They both looked as if they'd been sucking on dirty socks.

"Do they not know what time it is? It's eleven-frickin'-o'clock," Jacki groused. She glanced over at the mustached man who pointed across the hall. "Can you do something about this?"

Another burst of thuds. "You suck," the high-pitched voice screamed.

"You weren't complaining earlier, bitch," the man cackled.

"I know who they are," Austin whispered into Gina's ear. "It's Chad... with Harrison."

Gina covered her mouth to stymie a gasp of surprise. "Are you sure?"

Austin nodded, then scanned the hall again. "Look." He pointed to the ground outside the squabbling couple's door. There was a Bradley Prince Post-it note with a message scrawled on it.

Gina hurried and retrieved her phone. She opened the camera app and snapped a picture of the note. It read: YOU ARE NEXT!

"What does that mean? Next in line? Or is it a threat?" Gina asked.

"You're the bitch, bitch," came from the room.

With her hands on her hips, Jacki snapped, "That's it. I'm calling security. Ricky?"

"On it." Ricky disappeared into their room.

"Good. It's hard to sleep with that racket," a man said from down the hall. He nodded to Jacki and closed his door.

The mustached man hesitated a beat, but he too stepped back inside his room.

"I don't want to get stuck talking to the cops, again," Gina said with a frown. She and Austin retreated into his room, closing their door.

They monitored the fight through the walls. The security officer came and knocked on Harrison and Chad's room. After a few minutes of muffled discussion, the world returned to a quiet state.

"I didn't know Chad was gay," Gina said, pondering the argument they'd heard.

"It's news to me, too." Austin shrugged, running a hand through his gorgeous hair. "But I saw him leave the bar holding Harrison's hand."

"What notebook were they talking about?" she asked.

Austin shook his head. "I don't know, but I hope Chad isn't in trouble."

"This has to be related to Rodney's death. They mentioned his last name." Gina chewed her lip, took out her cell phone, and studied the photo of the threatening note.

Her phone pinged. It was a message from her sister.

Cyndi: *Are you alright? When are you coming back to the room?*

"What's up?" Austin asked, stepping up to Gina and pulling her into his arms.

"It's my sister. She's wondering when I'm coming back." Gina sighed, hiding a yawn. "I should probably go."

"I'm sorry tonight didn't turn out as I expected." He kissed the top of Gina's head and then released her. "Let me walk you to your room."

"You don't have to," Gina said, putting on her shoes.

"I told your sister I'd watch out for you."

"How about a compromise, then? Walk me to the elevator. We've got a long day ahead of us tomorrow." Gina took his hand and pulled him to the door.

As they waited for the elevator to arrive, he hugged her. She snuggled against his chest, regretting the decision to leave. Behind her, the cave-like elevator dinged, and the doors hissed open.

Austin released her. "Sleep well."

"You too." Gina stepped backward into the darkness. She couldn't pull her gaze from his amber eyes. She blindly reached for the buttons.

In her peripheral vision, a figure caught her attention. She turned and saw a man standing with his nose in the corner.

She reached out and touched his shoulder. "Sir, do you need help?"

"Gina, what's going on?" Austin's hand shot out to keep the elevator doors from closing.

The man shifted, his head turning Gina's way.

"Oh-my-God," Gina gasped, stepping back and clutching her chest. A purple author swag-pen stuck out of the man's neck and his mouth gaped open.

With every beat of her heart, the world moved in slow motion as the man fell toward her and pinned her to the floor.

"Ch–Chad." She stuttered in horror. His lifeless eyes stared down at her while blood dripped onto Gina. Her one arm was pinned, and the other felt like rubber. She kicked her feet, trying to get the body to roll. She couldn't breathe and panic set in.

All at once, time raced forward. Screams and the clanging alarm met her ears. Austin appeared over her, shoving Chad's body off and dragging Gina out of the elevator.

When their eyes met, Austin's face was stricken with horror.

A woman's voice cut through the emotional melee. "How can I help you?"

"Call 911," Austin yelled. "Someone was murdered."

There were gawkers in the hallway, three had their phones out.

"He's dead." Gina shook. Her body felt numb from the trauma.

"Are you okay?" Austin asked, holding her unsteady gaze.

"No," Gina laughed, refusing to release her hold on Austin. He scooped her up and carried her to the bench in the hall. He sat and rocked her.

A sob bubbled up from within, and she buried her face against his chest once more.

"Is she alright?" asked a feminine voice with a slight southern drawl. "The blood..."

"It's not hers," Austin was quick to say.

Gina leaned back and wiped the tears away. She glanced at her Boba Babes shirt covered in blood. Her shoes were ruined, too.

"Oh, Austin, it's everywhere. Gross. I'm sorry I got it on you." She struggled to stand, but he refused to let her go.

"Don't worry about me. Why don't you call Cyndi? She can bring clean clothes." Austin released her and Gina fished out her phone to dial her sister.

"Ello," Cyndi said in a groggy voice. "Do you know what time it is?"

"No." Gina stared vacantly. "He's dead," she whispered.

"Yeah, Rodney is dead. Tell me something I don't know." Cyndi huffed.

Austin leaned over and growled into the phone. "Cyndi, get to floor seven STAT. There's been another murder."

Chapter 8

Austin

A rush of people from their rooms crowded around us like a swarm of bees. Cell phones buzzed to life, poised to take pictures of the dead body half out of the elevator. I tried to pull Gina back toward my room, but her ramrod posture wouldn't be persuaded.

Her eyes were glazed in shock, and they remained on Chad's body. I had to get her out of here. With another tug, her watery eyes met mine before her feet did my bidding.

"Why? Who would do that to Chad?" Gina's words were as broken as her steps.

"I don't know, sweetheart, but when the cops get here, I'm sure we're going to find out," I sadly admitted, while leading her back to my room.

"I want my sister." Gina's voice hitched.

"She'll be here soon." I pulled her into the room, closed the door, and wrapped her in my arms. Gina shook as another choked sob left her lips. "Take deep breaths, sweetheart." I rubbed her back and hoped she would take in my calm.

Honestly, I was as far from composed, but I needed to remain steadfast for my girl.

Never in my life had I thought I'd see a friend and colleague's dead body. There was no doubt Chad was murdered. The quick proof was the purple pen sticking out of his neck and blood on the elevator floor and on Gina.

Looking at her bloody hand and clothes, she got the brunt of the clusterfuck this event had turned out to be.

Several loud bangs on the door made Gina jump from my embrace. "Open up, it's me, Cyndi."

Gina didn't hesitate and pulled out of my arms, racing to the door. The second it opened, the frustrated look on Cyndi's face didn't bode good news.

"First, you called me to get my ass up here with clothes, and then the damn elevator wasn't working. So, I had to climb three flights of stairs—which, by the way, I almost slipped on blood in the stairwell. Then, when I finally got up here, the frickin' elevator door opened, and a crowd of uniformed cops stormed out and started blocking off the area." She let out a warring breath before she continued. "Now who died?"

"The cops are here?" Gina asked, not picking up her sister's stress.

"Did you not hear me? Yes." Cyndi looked her sister up and down. Her eyes lasered in on the blood saturating Gina's clothing. "That's blood."

"No shit, Sherlock," Gina snapped.

Before I retorted, another knock came from the door. "Ms. DiCaprio, Mr. Blackmoor? This is Officer Cox."

I reached the door and quickly opened it. As much as I wasn't fond of the police, she was a welcome sight. "Come in. I was about to have Gina change."

"Then we caught you just in time. Ms. DiCaprio, since

your clothing needs to be added into evidence. Officer Jane will help you with the clothes. Is that alright?"

Gina nodded in silence. An officer, who stood behind Cox, moved past us with a large black kit and a plastic bag and led Gina into the bathroom.

"Can someone tell me who was murdered? And Austin, you better explain why my sister is covered in blood." Cyndi glared at me, hands on her hips, her eyes not blinking.

"Chad Cummings." It was all I could get out. The idea of my friend being dead hadn't sunk in.

"I'm sorry." Cyndi lost her frown, but a deep groove of regret settled between her eyes.

"Austin, can you tell me when you last saw Mr. Cummings?" Officer Cox asked as she pulled out a notebook and pen.

"Around nine o'clock. We were in the hotel bar."

"Did you see anything suspicious about him? Did he look worried or afraid?"

"No. None that I was aware of, but not long after Gina and I made it to my room, we heard shouting—arguing from the room next door. It sounded like Harrison and Chad, but I can't be exact," I explained.

"What were they arguing about?" Her pen poised to write.

"Not sure. It was mostly garbled, but we weren't the only ones who heard the argument. The guests around us came out of their rooms to listen. But you can call hotel security. They were notified."

"Don't forget the note," Gina added as she walked out of the bathroom with a towel around her. "Can I have my clothes, Cyndi?" Even though her question was directed at her sister, Gina's eyes were on me.

As she headed back into the bathroom, I took in her pale complexion and the tired expression on her face.

"That's right. There was a note on the floor in front of the arguing couple's door. It was written in red and said, 'You are next,' on a Bradley Prince's post-it note."

"A threat, possibly," Cox mumbled more to herself.

"I would see it as such," Cyndi commented gravely, but her eyes kept glancing over at the now-closed bathroom door.

"So, what happened after the fight?"

"Gina and I, umm... talked a bit more before I walked her to the elevator."

"You mean messed around," Cyndi chimed in with a knowing smirk.

"What time was that?" Cox asked, but she glanced at Cyndi with annoyance. "Please, Ms. DiCaprio, reserve your comments for the peanut gallery."

"Sorry. Calling a spade a spade, you know."

Officer Cox turned her back on Cyndi and refocused on me. "You were saying?"

"Around midnight."

"And then?" Cox prompted.

"I walked Gina to the elevator, the door opened, and the second she walked inside, Chad's body fell forward and landed on top of her. She screamed, and a mass of people came out of their rooms. It was sort of a blur from there."

Cox nodded, sympathy in her eyes. "Thank you. Now I need to talk to Gina. Would you mind if I have you and Ms. Di—"

"I'm not leaving my sister," Cyndi huffed. "I swear I will keep my mouth shut."

"Gina's rattled. I'd keep her sister here for Gina's sake," I admit. A large lump of guilt formed in my chest as worry for my girl stamped heavily in my mind. I promised Cyndi to protect her sister, and I didn't.

"Fine," Officer Cox relented.

Gina walked out of the bathroom and rushed over to me. "Don't go far." The stark look in her eyes reflected more worry. Worry I put there.

"I'll take the evidence down for processing," Officer Jane said and left.

"I'll be right outside those doors." Leaning down, I placed a gentle kiss on Gina's lips, then I walked out of the room, my feet just as heavy as my heart.

The cops were stationed around the elevator, while the hotel patrons were just beyond the yellow tape, taking photos and whispering.

"It's a shame," Duke Wain said with a shake of his head. "So young too. But drugs tend to lead these young folks on the wrong path."

I glared at the old man, who wrote westerns and World War II period pieces. What did he know about my generation? Nothing. "It is a shame alright. But Chad didn't die of drugs. He was murdered, Mr. Wain." I couldn't hide my contempt.

"Are you sure?" His eyes widened with shock. His question surprised me since Duke was there when I pulled Gina out from under Chad's lifeless body. He was close to the elevator. Didn't he see all the blood?

"Mr. Wain, someone stuck a pen in his neck," I explained with a little more vehemence. But I instantly regretted my tone. The man didn't know. "I'm sorry. Chad was my friend, and he wasn't a drug user. But..." I shake my head. "I still can't wrap my head around the fact that Chad is dead, and there's a murderer running around the hotel."

"I'm sorry, too. I didn't know he was your friend. I

know this is a terrible circumstance—two people were murdered. But I do love mysteries." He rubbed his hands together with agitation. "I wonder if the owl lady knows who killed your model friend and that terrible author?"

"What do you mean, the owl lady?" I tentatively leaned in slightly and took a sniff of the old man. He might have been talking about drugs, but alcohol could do the same thing. "Mr. Wain?"

"What?" He shifted his attention from the elevator to me.

"The owl lady?"

"Oh, yeah. After that whole ordeal with the argument earlier, I kept my eyes out through my peephole—just in case. And that was when I saw her."

"What did she look like?"

"I don't know." Duke twisted his mustache. "I couldn't see her face because it was covered by the hood. But she was wearing one-piece pajamas with large owls printed all over it."

"How tall was she?"

"She was short in stature—about here." Duke leveled a hand to his shoulder. "But it's weird because she looked like she came from that room." He pointed to Harrison's. "Why would she go in there? Harrison's gay."

"Are you sure she came from that room?" I asked, speculating..

"Yes. Too bad she was hiding her face under the hoodie. I'd love to know who she is."

"Mr. Wain, you need to tell the police. What if she's the killer?" I insisted, but the man shook his head. He was so serious in his denial.

"I'll wait to talk to Harrison first," he whispered. "What

if I was wrong about the girl? I don't want to be next on the killer's list." He was adamant.

"Mr. Blackmoor." Detective Burns called out my name as he strutted toward us. "Just the person I want to talk to."

"I already talked to Officer Cox about what happened." I crossed my arms and waited for some snide remark out of the blustering buffoon. In the back of my mind, I knew the cop was trying to do his job, but the way he handled himself was uncalled for. I had firsthand knowledge of how cops could roughly handle situations. Yet, this guy rubbed me the wrong way.

"You didn't talk to me, and I have some additional questions about how you can be a part of two murders within a day of each other."

He had me there.

"Well, Detective Burns, that's not really a question, is it?" Duke Wain asked, his brows high and tight, like his haircut.

"I would advise you to stay quiet if you don't want to get hauled to the station for questioning," Burns warned, pointing his finger at Duke.

Duke raised his hands in surrender, tight-lipped, and walked back to his room.

"Now you did it. He had possible information about Chad's murder," I accused, glaring at the detective.

"And you don't?" Burns eyeballed me with self-righteousness. "Maybe it would be best if we talk at the station."

Right then, my hotel door opened, and Gina, Cyndi, and Officer Cox stepped out.

"What's going on?" Gina asked as she reached my side and wrapped a possessive arm around my waist.

"The detective wants to bring me in for further questioning," I admit. My heart lurched at the thought of being in a police station. Even though it was only for questioning, I suddenly got a PTSD flashback from when I was seventeen.

"There's no reason for it. You didn't do anything wrong —he didn't," Gina insisted, putting herself in front of me. "We were together all night."

"Are you sure?" Burns countered in disbelief.

"Why would I lie?" Gina batted back with a frown.

"Detective Burns, may I have a word with you?" Officer Cox demanded, not giving him a chance to decline. She walked in the other direction of the hall.

The man mumbled something under his breath and stalked off toward Cox. Cyndi leaned in and whispered, "He's such a dick."

"No arguments from me," I said right back. Then I met Gina's eyes. "I'm not going anywhere."

"Good." Gina leaned up and planted a chaste kiss on my lips.

"Before you two get all gooey and such, I feel we need to do something about this situation. I don't want to live in this hotel for another week," Cyndi huffed out, planting a hand on her hip.

Gina turned to her sister. "What can we do?"

Then an idea struck me. "Duke Wain."

"The author?" Gina asked, as confusion crossed her brow.

"Yes. He saw someone dressed in owl pajamas, and he thinks they came out of Harrison's room."

"When?" she leaned deeper into me and whispered.

"He said after the fighting stopped. But I have a feeling he was holding something back."

"Then let's go talk to him before I keel over from lack of sleep," Cyndi insisted.

"But the cops need to know that bit of detail too," I added with a slight yawn.

"Why?" Gina chimed in. "It might have nothing to do with Chad's murder. Then again..." she looked at her sister and then at me. "It might."

Cox returned with Burns in her wake. "Ms. DiCaprio, earlier in the room, you said you overheard Harrison and another man arguing over something. Can you tell Detective Burns what they were arguing about?"

"We both heard it," I chimed in. "They were arguing about some notebook, and threats were uttered back and forth."

"Was that it?" Burns looked at me with a single brow of doubt.

"There was a note. Gina, can you show them the picture you took?"

"Sure," she said. Gina pulled her cell phone out and showed the detective the image.

"I think we need to have another chat with Harrison Busch," the detective announced. "Where's his room?"

Both Gina and I pointed to the door across the way.

"Step back." Burns turned to Cox and asked, "Are you ready?"

She nodded and followed him to the closed door.

They knocked several times before frustration won over the detective's face.

"I'll call the manager. She should be able to open it," Cox said as she pulled out her cell.

"In the meantime, you three head out of here. Just in case."

What does he think is going to happen? A shootout with Harrison? *Numb nuts.*

"We have every right to stand here," Cyndi chided, her

glare fiercer than a drag queen in a dance showdown.

With another withering look, Burns ignored us.

Not long after, Josey Wallace raced up with a keycard in hand. "Normally, we don't open the room unless we get permission from the occupant, but with a killer on the loose, we can't take any chances."

With one swipe, the lock disengaged, and Burns twisted the handle. Slowly, he pushed open the door, carefully looking this way and that. Cox just plowed past him, gun drawn and ready.

Not able to help our nosey selves, with Gina and Cyndi crowded at my back, we three looked inside the room and saw nothing but a disastrous mess—clothes were strewn about, sheets and blankets off the bed, the mattress itself off-kilter. The coffee maker had been thrown across the room.

"There's going to be an extra charge on Mr. Busch's card for all the damages," Josey huffed out.

But no Harrison.

"Is he in there?" Cyndi asked, which caught Officer Cox's attention.

"Okay, here's the deal." Cox waved her arms out, urging us to back out of the room. "This is an investigation, and that's a possible crime scene. You shouldn't be involved. Since this hotel and the guests are on lockdown until we see the surveillance video in the elevator and stairwell, I'd suggest y'all be on your best behavior and head back to your rooms. Got me?"

"Gotcha," all three of us said in unison.

Detective Burns curled his lip up in a sneer as he passed us with a cell phone to his ear. The asshole barked out orders as he approached the blocked-off elevator.

I felt a physical shiver from Gina and immediately looked down at my girl. "Are you alright?"

"I'm tired, but I'll be better once I get a stiff drink in me, and some sleep," she admitted, leaning on me.

"Then why don't you go with your—"

"No." She cut me off. "Stay with me."

"If you think—" Gina cut off Cyndi's tirade with a single glare. "Fine. Brandy's welcome in my room." Gina's sister's frown was deep.

My girl turned her beautiful blue eyes to me. "Please?"

How could I say no to that? "Yes. Let me get a change of clothes first."

I quickly grabbed my duffle and shave kit and met the girls back in the hallway.

"I think before we head to the room, we should talk to Mr. Wain," Gina suggested.

I took her hand in mine. "It's late. How about we talk to him first thing in the morning?" I countered, feeling the heavy exhaustion creeping into my system. From the not-so-steady footsteps of Gina and Cyndi, they needed sleep as well.

Since both elevators were shut down now, we had to take the stairs. Down one flight, I spotted a cop taking pictures of the blood splatter on a step. He looked up and ordered, "Don't touch the railings."

None of us uttered a word but nodded as we passed him and skipped over the bloody step. Once we made it to the fifth floor, we sped along the hallway until we got inside Gina's room.

After explaining to the girls what happened to Chad and the owl lady, we all decided to do a little investigative work for ourselves the following morning.

Brandy grabbed her things and went with Cyndi, which left Gina and me looking at each other.

"I can take this bed."

"No." Gina shook her head. "I want you to hold me."

"Are you sure?" I had to ask. "What about your sister and friends?"

"It's the surest thing I want right now," Gina quietly admitted, her attention fixed on the rug.

"Look at me, sweetheart," I said, caressing her cheek before pulling her into my arms.

"Just sleep." Her muffled words against my chest made me chuckle.

"I promise, just sleep."

Chapter 9

Gina

"Wakey, wakey, eggs and bakey," Sam hollered, entering the room like unwanted morning sunshine after a night of debauchery.

Gina groaned, keeping her eyes shut. Reluctant to leave her warm cocoon, she stretched. An arm tightened around her waist and her eyes popped open. Her chin rested on Austin's bare chest. She tilted her head so she could see his face. He blinked the sleep away and wore a half-smirk on his luscious lips. She grazed her fingers over his scruff.

How can a man look so sexy in the morning?

"I've had coffee delivered, y'all," Sam said in a singsong voice.

Gina groaned again and pulled the blanket over her head. "Go. Away."

Austin chuckled, vibrating Gina. She sighed. Staying in bed sounded way better.

"I didn't know what kind of coffee you liked, Austin, so I got a box of regular and all the fixin's from the Dilly Donuts coffee shop."

"Thanks, Sam." Austin stroked Gina's hair. Then folded down the covers. "Come on, sweetheart. Let's drink some ambrosia."

Cyndi burst into the room with a wry smile and damp hair. "Get up, you lazy asses. We've got murders to solve and a killer to catch. I'm pissed. They're talking about canceling the dang event. We can't let that happen." She put a paper cup under the coffee spout and pressed. Dark liquid streamed out, and a tantalizing aroma filled the room.

"Fine," Gina growled, images of the dead men popped into her mind. She slid her hand over Austin's abdomen, causing him to shiver. The smile on his face eased the burden of her thoughts.

"Later," he whispered into her ear.

"Okay," she agreed with hopeful excitement.

Sloth-like Brandy ambled to the coffee. All three women gathered around the table in Gina's room. Sam giggled, elbowing Cyndi. Their gaze swept the bed, landing on Austin.

A surge of jealousy filled Gina. She sat up and flung a pillow at the women. "Why the hell are you in here?"

Her friends and sister stared at her wide-eyed.

"Seriously? I have a sexy beast of a man in my bed, and you all storm in here for what—to get a good look at him?" She glared. "Coffee? You think I'd want that over him?"

"How about boba tea?" Brandy mumbled.

Gina shook her head, beginning to chuckle and defusing the moment.

Cyndi, Sam, and Brandy took their coffees and left the couple to dress. Gina showered and donned her new pink Boba Babes shirt to match the others. Austin commandeered the bathroom to shave while she applied her makeup near the window.

When the girls were dressed for the day, they ventured to the main floor.

As the elevator door opened in the lobby, the Boba Book Babes and Austin were assaulted with an onslaught of noise. Groups of people clumped around the seating areas or near the front desk and bar. The conversations caused quite the din that ebbed and flowed like a storm-battered shore.

The Boozy Book Bitches congregated near the bar entrance, holding plates of bagels slathered with cream cheese. Jacki had her arms crossed and her lips pursed while the others animatedly conversed in a tight circle.

"If they cancel I want my money back," one woman growled.

"This trip has been a disaster," another lamented. "Rodney Stiff is dead. I can't get all my books signed."

"Where's Harrison Busch, anyway?" Ricky asked, studying the lobby.

A woman with black readers glanced up from a paperback. "He's probably on the lam—"

"Or dead," Jacki said flatly.

"I hope not." Ricky frowned. "I thought he was cute."

"I thought he was sketchy," the woman with the readers said.

Cyndi led the way into the open lobby.

"Look," Gina nudged Brandy. The group came to a stop, and she directed their attention to a couple of authors under the chandelier in the center of the vast space. "Isn't that author LaShanda Rose speaking with Duke Wain?"

"Let's go talk to Duke," Cyndi said, stepping forward.

"Wait." Brandy shot her hand out and stopped her.

"The lady who checked us in is at the front desk working. She was very helpful when I asked about boba tea shops nearby. Maybe I can get some info from her."

The hotel employee in question glanced over at the Babes and smiled. Brandy raised her hand and wiggled her fingers in greeting. The young blonde blushed and quickly returned her attention to the older client at the counter.

"I'll tag along with Brandy," Sam said, starting toward the check-in desk. Brandy hurried after her.

Gina, Cyndi, and Austin weaved through the throng of sad, anxious, and mad people. They stopped short of the authors, deep in conversation.

"You know where he got the idea, don't you?" LaShanda conspired. She swung her head around before continuing. "Deidra Raines."

"You don't say." Duke smoothed his gray mustache. "That's a strong accusation. How do you know for sure?"

"She had an online class about researching and creating a captivating world for the readers. Rodney used her same exact words for towns, and he only switched the Cs for Ks in the word magic. He couldn't be bothered to attempt to hide the theft."

"Oh my," Duke gasped, clutching his chest.

"I swear he bastardized Bradley Prince's alien bride series by turning them into dragon shifters." LaShanda waggled a finger. "He stole whenever and whatever he could. All of his books are Frankenstein's monster of plagiarism. And then there's Jamison Blaine..."

"I heard rumors, of course." Duke nodded toward Deidra. "What did Deidra do about it?"

"There is a lawsuit, but I guess it doesn't matter since he's dead."

Gina turned to Cyndi. "That's why Rodney's series felt

so familiar. They were Bradley Prince's, wrapped up in a new world."

Cyndi shook her head. "I can't believe it. Rodney Stiff— a plagiarist?"

"If someone's stolen idea catapulted Rod Stiff into the limelight, and made him famous, then that person has a motive for murder," Austin surmised.

"Excuse me," Gina said to LaShanda. "I love your books, especially the *Elven Landscape* series."

"Thank you," LaShanda gushed. "It's always great to meet a fan."

"I overheard you speaking about Rodney, and I've heard the rumors. Is it possible he used your elvish word for semen in his dragon series?" Gina searched LaShanda's dark, stormy gaze.

"Yes. Yes, he did. Luckily, the dipshit stole from an older book. One of his beta readers alerted me, and I contacted my lawyer. By the time he agreed to change it, the book had already been published. It wouldn't have been a problem for him if he'd called the dragon's snot huhu'a, but the lazy ass used my word for his dragon semen." She shrugged. "Our readers crossover, so I wonder what he thought would happen?"

"Well, you don't have to worry about him anymore," Cyndi observed.

"That's true." LaShanda straightened and smiled. "Penelope Carter will be relieved, too."

"Oh, why's that?" Duke asked.

"Some of her notes disappeared after a panel discussion a year ago that included Rodney. Nothing can be proven, mind you, but Penelope had her suspicions about him back then." LaShanda shook her head. "It's all a big-fat shame."

Redd appeared beside Austin. He tugged on his elbow

and pulled him aside. His bloodshot, ice-blue eyes stared forlornly at him.

"Austin, have you heard? Do you think it's true?" Redd questioned.

Austin's gaze darted around, landing on Gina's face, then jumped back to Redd. "About what?"

"Chad." Redd's shoulders slumped forward like a beaten puppy.

The model's name gave Gina shivers. She remembered Chad's vacant green eyes before he toppled over her. He hadn't deserved to die so young.

"It's a fuck of thing to find out on Facebook." Redd's watery eyes hardened. He wiped his runny nose with the back of his hand.

"Yes, it's true." Austin met his eyes with a grim expression.

Redd turned crimson, and his gaze narrowed on Austin. "I thought we were friends. Why didn't you contact me about Chad?"

Cyndi approached the men, interrupting them. "The news is spreading about Chad's murder. It's almost as if it's a mystery dinner theater, the way these people are gossiping on social media."

"A favorite author and model has died, Cyndi. I'm sure most of them have read a whodunit or two. They'll want to help the only way they can, and that's unraveling the plot. Every murder has a plot," Gina said, rubbing Austin's arm. "I'm sorry about Chad, Redd."

Austin stiffened next to her at the mention of his friend. And Redd glanced across the room, wiping a rene-gade tear away.

"Can I have your attention, please?" Tammy said in a megaphone. The gathering quieted. "I need to clarify a few things. We have decided to continue with the book signing and Wizard of Oz after-party in honor of our sponsor, USA Today bestselling author Rodney Stiff and cover model Chad Cummings. All funds raised from the charity auction will be donated in Rodney and Chad's names. There's an updated schedule for today's events in our online group. Now, I'll turn it over to our illustrious Izzy Drummond."

Gina shared a stunned look with Cyndi.

"That's a surprise," Cyndi mumbled.

Izzy waved her arms, her blue and pink curls bouncing around her heart-shaped face. "Hey, everyone! I have some news about the charity raffle. The tables are set up in conference rooms A and B. Our authors and book clubs donated some fabulous prizes. Tickets are now on sale at the information table or grab a volunteer walking around the event. Go check the book baskets. They are fantabulous and so worth the money, including an evening with Jamison Blaine basket."

Cyndi gasped, grabbing Gina's arm. "Let's go."

Izzy rattled off more of the raffle gifts, and collectively the mass of readers headed toward the area with the items up for grabs.

"Hold on." Gina held Cyndi back, letting the throng pass.

Austin conferred with Redd in a low tone. But it was impossible to hear anything they said with the gaggle of women passing by.

"Brandy is waving at us," Cyndi said. "She wants us to come over."

Gina glanced at Austin. "I'll come with you," he said, shifting in her direction.

"It's okay. Your friend needs you, and I've got the Boba

Book Babes." She tiptoed and placed a kiss on his lips. He wrapped his arms around her, hugging her tight.

"I'll keep my eye on you," Austin said, releasing her.

Gina linked elbows with Cyndi, and they zigzagged their way around furniture and people to Brandy and Sam's side.

"Well?" Cyndi asked.

"Brandy's girl had a lot of info. I'm still trying to digest it all." Sam rubbed her temple.

"Becky told us about the surveillance video. She didn't see it herself, mind you, but overheard the officers talking about it. A person in owl pajamas boarded the elevator and sprayed the camera with red hair spray. They were hidden under the hood, so they couldn't be identified." Brandy's gaze shifted around the room.

"That sounds like premeditation to me," Cyndi offered.

Gina sucked in a breath. "What did Chad do—"

"Or what did Chad know?" Cyndi interrupted. Gina met her sister's eyes.

"I saw the person in the pajamas," Gina murmured. The image flashed in her mind.

"What?" her friends and sister said in unison. They leaned in closer.

Gina swallowed hard and nodded. "When Austin and I peeked into the hallway, listening to Harrison and Chad, I saw her walking toward the elevator. She must have been the one who dropped the note."

"Are you sure it was a woman?" Cyndi asked.

"Yes. The one-piece pajamas were pale blue with an owl pattern." Gina glanced across the lobby at Austin. He smiled and winked, causing the butterflies in her stomach to launch into a cyclonic dance. He was the shining light amongst the horror of the past twelve hours.

"Pale blue," Brandy echoed. "That's interesting."

"Yes. Becky said the officers couldn't determine the exact color because of the black and white footage," Sam added.

"But they thought it was possibly pale gray, tan, blue, or lavender." Brandy studied the blonde behind the counter. "Well, we can't do anything about it now. We should get some raffle tickets. I've got a lucky streak going at book events, and I need to fill my new bookshelf."

"You can win all the baskets, except one. Jamison Blaine's basket is mine." Cyndi put her hand on her hip.

Brandy smirked at the challenge. "I don't think so. It's up for grabs."

Cyndi growled, and Gina stepped between them. "Really? I can't believe you two biotches fighting over a basket you haven't even looked at yet."

"Alright." Brandy huffed. "Let's go this way. Becky showed me a shortcut." She pointed in the opposite direction Izzy had indicated.

"That makes perfect sense," Cyndi said, not budging.

"It circles around to the bathroom next to the conference area. Trust me. I know the shortcuts to the bathroom." Brandy straightened her shirt.

"Fine. Let me tell Austin—"

"Tell me what?" Austin appeared behind Gina, giving her a start.

"We are going to buy some raffle tickets, and they are opening the event for VIP holders soon," Cyndi offered, staring at the schedule on her phone.

Sam nodded. "Maybe we'll hear some more about Rodney's plagiarism—"

"Or the owl lady," Brandy added.

Austin glanced around the lobby, searching. "That

reminds me, we need to talk to Duke. He knows something about the owl lady. I don't see him now."

"He must be in the conference room," Gina said.

"Come on," Brandy motioned for them to follow. She headed toward the little used side exit, then turned into a narrow hallway. They passed a business center with a printer and a workspace. A metal door was at the end of the hall. As soon as Cyndi opened her mouth, Brandy took the handle and pushed the door.

Footsteps echoed on the concrete flooring. The brightly lit emergency stairwell was bare compared to the opulent lobby they'd just come from.

"This is the stairway the staff uses," Brandy explained.

"Do I want to know how you know this?" Cyndi asked, shaking her head.

"It's a shortcut." Brandy ignored Gina's sister's question and pointed to another gray steel door across the room. "Through there are the restrooms."

Housekeeping carts lined the wall, and a few were parked under the alcove. They shuffled past the eerie ascending stairs. Brandy pulled the door open a crack, lighting the dismal gray stairwell.

Gina threw a glance over her shoulder at the carts. She gasped.

"What's wrong?" Austin glanced around.

She pointed with a shaky hand. "Do you see it?"

Sam started forward. "What in Sam Hill?"

A wad of baby blue fabric poked out from a cart in the back.

"Don't touch anything," Austin warned.

Sam nodded. Using a washcloth from another cart, she lifted the blue item. "Good grief, y'all. I've found the owl doohicky."

Gina clutched Austin's arm. "We need to call Officer Cox."

Austin pulled out the card and his phone, then texted the cop.

Sam leaned over the dirty laundry basket with a crinkled nose. "It's nasty—wait. There's something else. It looks like paper." She carefully extracted the scrap.

They all pushed close to get a better look. The pink paper had blood splatters on it. Gina tried to focus on the handwriting and not on the blood.

The door burst open. "Nobody move!" A tall, muscular cop ran in, weapon drawn and pointed at them.

Chapter 10

Austin

Three more cops stormed in, guns raised and shouting, "Freeze!"

"Fuckity, fuck, fuck, fuck," Brandy spat out as she took a step backward and knocked into Sam. She dropped the washcloth, and the paper flitted to the top of the dirty linen pile.

"Put those guns down," Officer Cox called out as she strode into the area. Everyone was talking at the same time. She gave a shrill whistle and got the girls' attention.

I let out a breath and pointed to the owl pajamas. "Guess what we found?"

Cox looked down, a crease cutting between her brows. "John," she called over her shoulder, "Grab the evidence kit."

"Be right back," he said and took off.

"Who touched what?" Cox asked, looking at each of our faces.

"Nobody touched the pajamas." Gina raised her hand. "I lifted it with a towel then found a bloody piece of paper, which I dropped back inside the laundry cart when the GI Joes stormed in here and scared the crap out of us," Sam growled.

"Then step away, and let me look at it," Cox ordered. She leaned in and scanned inside the container.

We did as she said and John rushed in with a black bag. He pulled out a set of gloves and a plastic bag and handed them to Cox. She reached in, retrieving the owl one-piece and put it in the bag. Then she carefully picked up the note while John pulled out a smaller baggy. He opened it, and Cox slipped the paper inside.

"What happens next?" I asked Cox, as Gina yawned and leaned into me. I wrapped my arms around her and pulled her close. "Are you tired?"

"Just a little. Didn't sleep well last night," Gina admitted with another small yawn, then turned to Officer Cox. "Did you find Harrison yet?"

"No. It looks like he just disappeared. However, he left his stuff in his room, so I'm hoping he comes back to get it, and then we can catch him."

"What did you find, Officer Cox?" Detective Burns strode in and stared at each one of us with a hostile glint, like we interrupted his donut break.

"The pajamas and a piece of paper with writing and blood on it. It might be linked to the model's murder," she said as she studied the paper through the evidence bag.

"Well, I got some news dealing with the video surveillance taken from the elevator." Detective Burns turned to us and ordered, "I want to see all your right wrists."

"What for?" Cyndi asked with a bit of venom.

"Show me your wrists, and I'll explain," he pushed, pointing at Cyndi first.

"Here's mine," I said, exposing my wrist covered with a thunderbird tattoo honoring my mother's Chippewa heritage.

"So, the killer has a tattoo on their right wrist? Is that what you're saying?" Brandy chimed in while, exposing hers.

"Pull up your sleeve." Burns leaned in and studied Brandy's black and white tattoo of books and a teapot.

"Want to kiss my hand while you're at it?" Brandy snatched her hand away from the detective's glower. "I did not kill anyone. I was with my friends the entire time."

"Don't worry. It's not the right tattoo."

"So, Brandy is correct that the killer has ink on the right wrist?" Cyndi chirped as she pulled up her sleeve and exposed the moon and sun tattoo on her forearm. "I think this is sitting too far back."

Burns grunted and examined Gina's wrist, which was void of any ink. "I can't give out the details, but we did capture something on the video feed. But that's all I'm going to say."

"You pretty much told them what we're looking for," Cox muttered under her breath.

"If we're done here, we're going to look at the raffle prizes," I said as I looked at my girl. A frisson of excitement coursed through me to call her mine.

"Fine, but if we have questions, we will call on y'all," Burns belted out.

"We aren't going anywhere," I retorted while eyeing Cox, who was shaking her head.

Once in the main lobby, Cyndi turned to us with a half-cocked grin. "I think we should scan the baskets first, then head to the room for the wagon. Since the signing isn't until later, I think Austin should go with Gina for a nap, just in case, for protection." She triple-winked at her sister, which pulled a smile out of her.

Jesus, can Cyndi be more obvious?

"That sounds awesome, but I have to work soon," I said with disappointment.

"A quick look at the baskets sounds great," Gina declared as she took my hand and led me to the back area of the room where the raffle baskets and items were on display.

There were two rows of tables in the center and four tables flanking the ends. Baskets full of books, mugs, and swag, wrapped in clear cellophane, and several other miscellaneous items were up for the raffle. Gina and I went one way while Cyndi, Sam, and Brandy started on the other side.

Half a row down from us, a woman began to yell her head off and pointed to a basket she stood in front of. "That can't be blood. No way. Tammy!" she screeched.

A bunch of us rushed over and looked inside the basket. Sure enough, there was a pen covered in blood, laying haphazardly next to a box of chocolates and a fluffy white and black checkered blanket.

Blood drained from Gina's face as she stared at the pen.

"Don't look at it, Gina." I turned her away from the table.

"Is it the same kind of pen that killed Chad?" The rough edge of her words urged me to gather her into my arms. I want nothing but to protect her from what's happening at this event.

"Don't touch a thing. Step back," Detective Burns shouted as he raced over, with Cox right on his heels.

"John," she called out.

"On it," the officer responded and ran over with gloved

hands. He pulled out the camera and took pictures of the basket and the bloody pen. Once he got every angle, John grabbed a small empty bag out of the kit. He carefully picked up the pen, dropped it in, and sealed it. Then he picked up the basket and walked out of the event room.

"Did you see whose basket that was?" Sam asked as she tried to peer at the tag on the tabletop.

"I don't know, but from the glimpse of the back cover, I'm pretty sure it's one of Deidra Raines'," Brandy said as she stared at the basket closest to her. "Cyndi, look at this. It's Jameson Blaines'." She waggled her brows.

"Well, he's not here to ogle at." Gina stepped away from my embrace and elbowed her sister. Then a small round of laughter from the women had me chuckling.

Thank goodness for Brandy's sense of humor.

"Would you all just shut up," Cyndi hissed.

Screaming in the hallway had me moving with the Boba Book Babes shadowing me. Jacki, the head of Boozy Book Bitches, and her right-hand man, Ricky, were standing by the entrance, arguing with the detective and Officer Cox.

"We were set up," Jackie screeched in Burns's face.

"I swear, we would never kill anyone, especially with a pen," Ricky said, wrapping his arms around his middle. "We might be mean, but we're honest."

As the scene unfolded, Detective Burns stared intently at Ricky's enfolded arms. "Let me see your wrist." He pointed to Ricky.

"Why?" Jackie stepped in front of her friend and blocked the cop from reaching him.

"If you don't want to go to jail for impeding in a double murder investigation, I'd suggest you get out of my way."

The stern warning tone from the detective was enough for Jackie to move aside. "Now, Mr. Sparks. Your wrists."

With tears streaming down his face, Ricky unfolded his arms and exposed both wrists to Burns.

"Officers, arrest Mr. Sparks for the murder of Chad Cummings," Detective Burns announced.

Ricky's shrill could be heard throughout the hotel's main floor as two uniformed officers handcuffed him, read the Miranda, and took him away.

"He's innocent," Jackie bellowed, racing out the glass doors behind the cuffed Ricky.

As much as I found that group rude and belligerent, Ricky was far from being a killer.

Cox's gaze was on the doorway. "I can't believe it."

"What don't you believe?" I asked, looking out the glass door where Jackie was running after the patrol car Ricky was in. The familiar reporter and her camera man ran after them, her microphone shoved in Jacki's face.

"Ricky didn't do it. I saw the tattoo in the video surveillance and it doesn't resemble the shape of what that kid has." Cox walked away, muttering something I couldn't hear.

I shook my head and then turned to the girls. "Are you ready for some fun for a change?"

Gina nudged me and whispered, "That's for later."

Chapter 11

Gina

Gina clung to the VIP bag hanging on her shoulder. Austin held her hand while talking to a couple of readers. Brandy pulled her wagon as the Boba Book Babes inched forward in the line.

"We already checked in," Sam groused, looking around the group toward the uniformed officer and the event volunteers at the ballroom entrance.

Tammy sashayed over to Austin. "Hey, you tall, dark, delicious drink of bourbon. Since you won't be promoting for Rodney Stiff today, Molly Caudill suggested you go to Deidre Raines' table. You're on a few of her covers, right?" She skimmed her talons down his arm.

Bitch. Gina remained stoic, although she wanted to scratch Tammy's eyes out.

Austin stepped backward, breaking contact with Tammy. "Okay. I'll see what she wants me to do."

Tammy's gaze flicked to Gina, then back to Austin. She leaned close to him as if sniffing freshly baked bread. "Have you seen Redd? Penny Buttons would like him there to promote *Taking the Highlander by the Hilt.*"

"I saw Redd in the lobby earlier. I don't know what happened to him." Austin peered around the area, seeking his friend. "I can text him."

"You'd do that for me?" With a hand on her chest, Tammy batted her lashes. "Thank you. I won't forget this."

"Oh, brother." Gina rolled her eyes.

Austin tapped the screen of his phone. He texted Redd. "Done."

"You're awesome," Tammy gushed.

A gray-haired woman in a royal blue volunteer shirt hurried over to the hostess. Her name tag read Ruby in blocky letters. She raised her hand. "Excuse me."

Tammy huffed. "What do you need, Ruby? And put your hand down."

"Where are the extra raffle tickets? We are getting low."

Austin turned his back to Tammy and met Gina's gaze. "I guess I need to work." He tugged her into his embrace and nuzzled her hair, breathing in deeply.

An ache crept into Gina's chest as she contemplated their separation. "Be careful," she murmured. "The killer has already murdered one model." She squeezed him tight, tilting her head and claiming his lips.

He ended the kiss and walked off. She sighed, biting her lower lip.

With hands on her hips, Tammy mumbled, "he's mine."

Before Gina could respond to that preposterous claim, excited murmurs from the attendees drew her attention toward the front of the line. The ballroom doors swung open, signaling the start of the event. The VIP readers carried bags and carts full of books to be signed and empty totes ready to fill with pre-ordered novels.

"Where do we go first?" Sam asked, holding the event map upside down.

"Not there." Brandy pointed to the first table as they entered the crowded event room. "We'll start at the back and work our way around to avoid the clog at the front."

"Makes sense." Sam nodded and righted the map. She followed Brandy and the wagon as they weaved through the aisles toward Keeley Wetstone's table.

"Good morning," the youthful author said. "I write young adult and new adult paranormal and contemporary stories."

"I know," Brandy grinned with exuberance.

Cyndi led Gina up to the table. They perused the book covers and swag. Little fairy lights twinkled on the tablecloth.

"Brandy probably pre-ordered a series," Cyndi whispered to Gina.

"Wanna bet?" Gina said, covering her mouth so Brandy wouldn't see her talking. Her friend usually didn't go for young adult books. Brandy liked her stories hot—the spicier and kinkier, the better.

Cyndi's brows shot heavenward. "How much?"

"Ten tickets toward the Jamison Blaine raffle."

"You're on. Series versus a single book. She buys a series, I win. If she only pre-ordered a single book, you win." Cyndi stuck out her hand.

Gina shook it, and they turned to watch Brandy and Keeley interact.

"I've got the first in your Coven series. It's really good, and I loved when the hero was turned into a toad. I pre-ordered the second."

"Great!" Keeley clapped her hands.

"Shiitake mushrooms." Cyndi crossed her arms.

"Would you mind signing these VIP bags?" Sam asked, offering a collection of rainbow permanent markers for Keeley to choose from.

As Keeley signed Brandy's book and the bags, Gina searched for Austin amongst the sea of banners. She found Deidre Raines' logo against the sidewall toward the front. She sighed; the Boba Book Babes had a slew of authors to visit before reaching her Philly.

After walking the aisles, meeting new authors, and buying a few books or reader trinkets, they found themselves at Addie Werner's table. The purple-haired paranormal author was seated, signing a stack of novels.

"Her shirtsleeves look like tattoos," Sam said while they waited their turn.

"Those are tattoos," Gina replied. "Detective Burns wouldn't like her wrists."

"Too much ink," Cyndi agreed, nodding.

The other readers left Addie's table satisfied. Brandy stepped up. "Hi, I pre-ordered the entire Vampire Bride series."

Gina met Cyndi's gaze and shrugged.

"God bless America," Cyndi growled. "I picked the wrong author to bet on."

"You've won my pre-order giveaway," Addie exclaimed to Brandy, pulling out a large canvas bag with a vampire fangs logo.

"Sweet." Brandy grinned and shifted books in her wagon. "I have a few other books for you to sign."

"I have a pre-order too," Gina offered, reciting her name. "I was looking forward to hearing you speak at the paranormal talk."

Addie's gaze jumped to Gina's face. "I was looking forward to it as well. It's too bad. Karma's a bitch." She retrieved Gina's paperback and tucked a bookmark inside.

Gina shared a look with Sam, Brandy, and her twin. Karma didn't target Rodney, the killer did.

Brandy snagged a chocolate. The readers next in line pressed close as Sam picked up the signed bags. "Next," Sam said, waving the bags.

Penny Buttons had thrown a tartan plaid over her table. She was dressed in a Scottish historical dress with a cream bustier and a red plaid skirt. Her long strawberry blonde hair rested in ringlets around her heart-shaped face.

Redd wore a fitted black t-shirt and kilt. He looked dashing, but the smile on his chiseled face didn't reach his eyes. Penny's fans surrounded him. They held recently purchased books and wanted pictures with him.

While Redd appeared able to heft a sword and single-handedly defeat the marauding Viking invaders, his face was splotchy. But it could have been the lack of sleep, stress, or his ginger complexion. Gina figured it was the result of Chad's death.

The Babes glanced at the table, but highlander historicals weren't their preference. Even so, they considered the swag. "Men in kilts is my mom's guilty pleasure," Brandy giggled, "especially on a windy day."

Cyndi shook her head. "Let's go see Duke Wain."

Gina glanced past the end of Penny's display shelf. The coordinators hadn't removed Rodney's Stiff's table. A black tablecloth shrouded the piles of merchandise, a grim reminder of the murder.

A few readers took pictures of Rodney's banner. Others ignored it and focused on the surrounding authors.

Gina slowly pulled the wagon while Brandy had a book

signed by Penny. Sam caught up with Gina and set the bags and markers in the cart.

Sam rolled her shoulders. "I don't get why y'all get every stinkin' author to sign those bags or other things." She motioned toward a couple of readers. They wore event shirts with dozens of signatures.

Gina recognized Austin's name on the one woman's sleeve. She wanted to rush through the crowd to his side but shook the fanciful idea from her head. Austin had a job to do, and she'd paid for the event, even though she'd experienced more than she'd bargained for. Might as well enjoy what she could.

"It's an easy souvenir." Gina shrugged. "Sometimes an indie author goes big, and we'll have their signature."

"It's too bad about Stiff. Now that he's dead, I suppose his signature will be worth something.." Sam's face crinkled as she studied the black-draped table.

A balding, uniformed officer stood behind Rod's area. His gaze roamed the aisle, bouncing from one participant to the other. Rodney's image glared from his banner accusingly at all who passed. The air suddenly felt heavy.

Sam touched Gina, startling her. "Are you okay?" she asked, concern creasing her delicate brow.

Gina nodded, inhaling deeply. "It's so sad."

"I know." Sam waved her hand. "We should've gone to Fortuna, Texas. Their shenanigans would have been quite different from Peoria's."

Gina jerked her head up and stared wide-eyed at her friend. "Holy hell, Sam. I didn't think you'd read the article because it was about romance books."

"Listen, Gina. I don't read most of the book reviews or author updates that all y'all post in the group chat, but the Fortuna link had such an awesome clickbait title: *Officer*

Who Acts Out Scene Thrown in Slammer. Add a partially fuzzed-out picture of a hot, seemingly-naked dude... that's my kind of shenanigans. The guy wasn't an actual policeman but was acting out a love scene for his sweetheart. It was romantic and hilarious. I like that town. I think I could get into romance novels if my future man read them to me. He'd earn bonus points for dressing up and acting out a scene or two."

"Wow. Maybe you should check the Fortuna singles' ads," Gina teased.

Sam's jaw dropped open, then snapped shut. The girls giggled.

"Look." Cyndi appeared at their side.

She pointed at the crowd gathering around Duke's table, where a reporter stuffed a red-tipped mic in his face. The camera light threw shadows, making the banners seem twelve feet high. Duke fiddled with his bolo tie while offering the Barbie-look-alike reporter a half-hearted grin.

"Let's get closer so we can hear." Cyndi closed the distance. Gina and Sam followed her. Brandy met them with her recent package in hand.

"Don't you need to pick up something for your dad?" Brandy asked Gina.

"That's right. Thanks for reminding me."

"What did you get?" Cyndi asked.

"I bought Dad Duke Wain's latest western for Christmas."

"I wish I would have thought of it." Cyndi tiptoed toward the offerings on Duke's tabletop.

"So, Mr. Wain, what inspires your stories?" the reporter asked.

"I find inspiration everywhere, Ms. Fitzpatrick," the author replied.

"What about this book, *Murder at Midnight?*" The reporter held a novel, displaying it for the cameraman to focus on. The dark cover had a cowboy holding a knife dripping blood, which glinted in the full moon.

"Well, I, uh... it was–"

"Based on a real-life murder?"

"Yes. A robbery along a stagecoach trail inspired the idea," Duke started. He smiled and delved into the story premise. "The main character is an anti-hero modeled after a real-life robber turned vigilante. He was an 1800s version of an American Robin Hood cowboy."

The reporter's eyes glazed over a moment until they refocused on Rodney Stiff's table. "That sounds fascinating, doesn't it, folks?"

The crowd cheered, and Duke turned crimson.

"What's next, Mr. Wain? Are you going to incorporate an author's murder into a new book?"

Duke's face paled. His gaze slid around the room. "I think it's in poor taste to talk about the deceased so soon, Tanya."

The reporter ignored him and moved to the next question.

"I didn't know he wrote true life crime," Cyndi whispered.

"Me either," Gina replied. "I wonder if all his stories are based on historical events?"

Brandy shrugged. "It does make me want to find out more about his work."

"How does he research stuff?" Sam asked.

"He finds things in old newspapers," a soft raspy voice said next to them.

The Boba Book Babes turned and found Molly there. She cleared her throat, looking unsettled as she pushed up her red-rimmed glasses. She shifted and offered, "I've done some research for authors."

"That's cool," Brandy smiled.

"Do you find stuff for a lot of authors?" Sam asked.

Molly gave a one-shoulder shrug. "Sometimes. I have a knack for finding the macabre. You just have to know where to look."

"Macabre. That's cool," Brandy echoed.

"What's the creepiest stuff you've researched?" Sam asked, intrigued.

Molly's shy grin turned wicked. "Ever or recently?"

"Ever," Brandy said.

"Recently," Gina inquired at the same time.

Molly giggled and leaned in. "Well, don't tell Deidra this, but Addie Werner asked me to do some research for her vampire series. She wanted to know how long it would take for an adult man to bleed out from various wounds. You know, all different things like getting a leg hacked off to stabbed in the heart—"

"Or jugular," Cyndi muttered under her breath.

Gina shuttered, envisioning poor Chad.

"It was pretty gruesome work," Molly continued, "But I've researched many ways to kill people for Deidra and other authors. Even Rodney Stiff." Darkness covered her features. She blinked and cleared her throat again. "I've never researched for Duke, though."

"How do you know about the newspapers, then?" Cyndi asked.

Molly's gaze jumped to Cyndi. "Harrison Busch told me about his technique."

"Are you and Harrison chummy?" Gina questioned with a raised brow.

Grimacing, Molly's razor-sharp gaze narrowed on

Gina. "No. Just because we are both personal assistants for notable authors doesn't mean we are friends. He's a slimy eel who'd rather coax info out of people and steal it than do his own research." It seemed Rodney and his PA were both disliked.

Gina considered Molly in a new light. *Could this tiny woman be a suspect?*

She met her sister's gaze and concluded the Boba Book Babes needed to discuss Molly and how she fit into the murders.

Chapter 12

Austin

Between signing books, shirts, and other swags, I attempted to keep an eye on my girl. But Gina kept disappearing into the crowd of readers. Even with the murder of Rodney and Chad, these voracious readers wouldn't be stopped from seeing their favorite authors.

I spied Redd from two rows away. He looked miserable. His face was blotchy, and his red-rimmed eyes were still watery. If I was Penny Buttons, I'd send Redd away with his dour and dreary demeanor. He wasn't helping her out at all.

"I think I'm done with you," Deidra announced as she threw down the pen and rubbed her at her hand. There was an hour left before the signing ended. "It's not as busy as usual. And we know why?" Her remark was as sharp as a pointed blade.

"Are you sure you don't want me to stay longer?"

She glanced beside me, a tiny thin grin on her pixie face. "I think you have a visitor."

I turned as Gina strode up with a brilliant smile.

"Did you miss me?" She tipped onto her toes and kissed me generously in front of all who could see. "I missed you."

I pulled her tighter to me and tasted her sweet lips. "I did miss you."

Someone gagged behind us. We both turned and saw Tammy, with a hand on her throat, pretending to retch.

"Ignore the bitch," Deidra said with a snap of her fingers. "Why don't you two get out of here?"

"Sounds like a plan to me." Gina gave me a squeeze before she led me out of the signing.

Outside the event room, I pulled her short. "Where are your sister and friends?"

"The Babes are going to try to find out more about Molly and her association with Rod Stiff–but I'll explain that to you later. I'm done," Gina announced as she leaned against me again. "Take me up to your room." For the first time, I noticed her eyes were bloodshot. There was a hint of dark shadowing under them. But there's also a spark in her blue depths.

"Whatever you want, sweetheart." I squeezed her tight to me. "Are you hungry? We can get something to eat and bring it up."

"I told the girls we'll meet up with them around two for lunch," Gina said as they headed toward the elevator.

"That's a good idea." I smiled.

I pushed the up button, and the door opened right away. After she pressed seven, we quietly stood hand in hand with our own thoughts.

We remained quiet through the hallway until my hotel room door had shut. Then she was on me. "I can't wait, Philly," she confessed. "Kiss me."

With the drapes still drawn, only a hint of light came from between the cracks. I didn't get a chance to turn on the light either, as she jumped into my embrace and clasped her arms around my neck.

I didn't hesitate and supported her weight, cradling her ass in my hands. Her legs automatically wrapped around my waist. We were eye to eye before I kissed her crazy.

"Gina," I groaned, wanting more of her than I wanted to admit.

In-between the ravaging kisses, she slid down my body, and we took our clothes off like two unhinged nudists. I left on my boxers while Gina had on her bra and panties. They were a matched set, all lacy white and satin pink.

A single glance down her body and my need ramped up. I was desperate to be inside this woman—my woman. But I had to take it slow. This was Gina. Beautiful, soft, and sexy Gina. Full breasted, slender hips, and long legs–I wanted to touch her everywhere.

We ripped the top coverlet and sheet off the bed, and climbed onto the mattress. The feeling of her gorgeous body melding into me made my dick rock hard.

"Touch me, Austin," Gina whispered in the dark.

Between the coaxing of her luscious mouth and the heat of her body, I couldn't deny Gina of what she wanted.

I shifted slightly off of her, caressing along her shoulder to her right breast. With a soft knuckle-graze along her tight nipple, she arched, wanting more. Releasing her mouth, I trailed along her jawline, kissing every inch. All the while, my hand cupped her full mound.

The moment I reached her breast, I pulled back the thin lacy fabric with my fingers and sucked her pert pink tip into my mouth. Gina groaned, which spurred me to coax more of the sexy sounds out of my girl.

With the gentle nips and flicks of my tongue, I softly trailed my hand down the side of her torso to the thin trim

satin of her panties. She shivered. My name on her lips was a parting invitation to keep going.

I traced the edge of her panties until my fingers dipped inside and found her wet and wanting. With a hungry growl, I seized possession of her mouth, while my digits played with her sensitive bundle of nerves. I took every last moan Gina sang until she cried out my name and climaxed in my arms.

It didn't matter if I was still hard as granite. Knowing Gina got gratification had me almost releasing myself like a prepubescent teen in his first wet dream.

"Oh, *my* God, Austin," she cooed, her eyes full of desire. "Now it's your turn."

Before I got a word out, there was a knock on the door.

"No way," Gina complained. She grabbed my head and pulled me in for more kisses. "Ignore them. They will go away."

More knocks came, which turned incessant.

"I gotta get it, baby." I climbed off the bed and stomped to the door. I peered through the peephole. "It's Redd, and he looks like crap."

Gina tossed my jeans. I snagged them out of the air, and quickly slid them over my boxers. She got off the bed and hastily dressed.

I opened the door and immediately saw bloody knuckles on both of Redd's hands.

"I'm sorry, but I need someone to talk to." Redd burst out crying, walking into the room.

Gina gave a sympathetic glance to Redd, and then at me. "I'll grab some ice for his hands." She picked up the ice bucket and left the room.

I let out a resolved breath and knew what Redd was about to tell me wasn't good news.

Chapter 13

Gina

After retrieving a bucket full of ice, Gina handed it to Austin. "Is he okay?" she whispered.

"I don't think so. Something is wrong." Austin glanced into the room.

Gina reached out, touching his arm. "He needs a friend. I'll find my sister."

"But—"

"I'll be fine." Gina kissed his cheek. "I'll text you when I find them."

A sob bubbled up from Redd. He blew his nose, sounding like an elephant trumpeting.

"Just be careful."

"I'll be damned if I let someone off me by lame swag. It's got to be gilded or, even better, solid gold, not plastic." She slipped away with a wink.

"At this point, no swag is good swag."

Waiting nervously for the elevator, she heard someone cough in the hallway. She stiffened, ready to scream bloody hell. Then Duke Wain strolled around the corner.

She blew out a relieved breath.

"Hel-loo, little missy. How are you faring?" Duke's gray mustache twitched as he smiled. He pushed the call button even though it was already lit.

"I don't know, honestly." Gina shrugged, and her chest tightened, recalling the confines of the elevator. *God, I hope nothing else pops out of there.*

Duke touched her arm, studying her face. "It's been a helluva weekend."

Gina jumped away, then swallowed hard, her heart in her throat. Her eyes narrowed on Duke's weathered face. Cyndi's voice intruded into her mind. *He's a suspect, biotch. Get away from him.*

"Your clandestine weekend with your beau isn't turning out as you had planned?" he asked.

"I hadn't planned on meeting him, only Rodney Stiff," Gina said, envisioning Austin's luscious body in tight boxer briefs and his hands all over her.

Duke's brows rose over his wide eyes, giving him an owl-like appearance. *Stupid, ı need to question him.*

"Can you describe the person you saw outside of Harrison's door?" Gina asked.

Duke blinked a few times. "Yes," he drawled.

The elevator pinged, and the doors slid open. She stared into the empty space, frozen. Only when Duke breezed past her did her feet loosen enough to move. "Lobby please," Gina asked.

He pressed the button. Suddenly, the small space filled with cologne like her grandpa used to wear. She fought the urge to cover her nose. The elevator jerked to a start, and she panicked.

To distract herself, Gina focused on grilling Duke about the mysterious *owl lady.* "What exactly did you see?"

"I've already told everything to the police." He pressed his lips into a firm line and stared at the door.

"Please, Mr. Wain. Harrison's room is next to my boyfriend's room," she insisted. "I need to know the killer isn't after Austin. And the owl lady might have information to help." She locked her fingers together as if begging. "Please."

Duke sighed but nodded as the doors opened. He stepped into the lobby but called over his shoulder. "Follow me."

They headed into the bar. Duke ordered a top-shelf bourbon. "Want anything?" he asked as they sat on plush stools.

"No, thanks." She pointed toward the main desk. "I'm meeting my sister for lunch."

As Gina waited for Duke to talk, she sent a text to Austin, then to the Babes group chat. After a few sips, the alcohol loosened his lips.

"About the lady I saw—"

"Are you sure it was a lady? They've arrested Ricky the Boozy Book Bitch. The scrawny guy in the room next to you."

"That twerp?" Duke laughed. "I can see why they thought it was him, but no..." He took another swig. "It was a woman. I saw her profile."

Gina gasped. "You saw her face? Who is it?"

Duke turned crimson. He stared into the amber liquid as if hoping it would answer for him. "Not her face, her bazookas."

Gina chuckled. "Really?"

"Not on purpose. It just happened. I opened the door to get ice. I didn't know what she was until she turned. She was bent over, putting that paper on the ground. The hood covered her face and hair, but her chest poked out a bit." He rubbed his chin. "I suppose it could've been a man, nowadays."

"Bazookas," Gina reiterated, quietly giggling.

Duke's lips twisted into a smirk. He shrugged, fingering his drink. Suddenly, Duke jumped. "It was a woman, by God. The owl pajamas didn't have feet, and she wore slippers without socks. She had boney ankles with something blue on one."

"Blue as in jewelry–like an anklet? Or a blue tattoo?" Gina asked, remembering the woman in the bathroom before Rodney's death.

Duke blinked, tilting his head. "I don't know. I was focused on her—"

"Bazookas. Yeah, I get it." Gina hopped up. "Thanks for sharing with me. I need to find my sister."

Gina hurried through the posh lobby. LaShanda Rose sat next to Penny Buttons on a plush sofa.

LaShanda spoke to a frail woman with an oxygen tank, handing her a basket. "Thank you for staying after all that's happened, Julia," the author smiled. "Congratulations on winning my table giveaway. I hope you like it. There's a new water bottle with my complete series."

"Thank you. I loved *Knickers in a Bunch,* and I can't wait to read the second in the series," the reader said as she glanced into the basket.

"I hope you like *Drawers on the Floor* just as much." LaShanda patted her arm.

Gina smiled as she passed. *I love reader and author events.*

She pressed her lips together and increased her speed, determined to find her friends. She rounded the long hallway leading to the conference rooms. Sam and Brandy stood next to a pile of stuff.

"I need to find LaShanda Rose. I forgot to get her signature for this anthology," Brandy said, unzipping her boba tea backpack and retrieving the thick paperback.

With her hands on her hips, Sam huffed. "How many signatures did you miss this time?"

"Only ten."

"Only ten." Sam harrumphed.

Not fazed, Brandy glanced at a list of author signatures she needed. She looked up, seeing Gina.

"Darn it. I forgot to get my anthology signed, too," Gina lamented.

Sam threw her hands up. "Whatever y'all. I can't rationalize getting into all these books."

"Not even if you're spending your evenings between the covers with book models?" Gina teased.

"Speaking of book models... That was a short *nap*." Brandy wiggled her brows.

"Unfortunately, the napping was interrupted by another distraught model," Gina frowned, recalling Redd's tear-stained face.

Brandy hummed. "Sounds like the beginning of a reverse harem and something I'd read."

"Where's Cyndi?" Gina asked, completely ignoring her friend.

"Going gaga over some author's basket," Sam answered, rolling her eyes.

Brandy slipped her backpack on and leaned close to Gina. "It's the Jamison Blaine package."

Gina shook her head. "Geesh."

"Actually, it's an awesome package. You get a night out with Jamison, a bunch of premium swag, like a pair of engraved wine glasses, an expensive bottle of wine, dinner at a swanky place, and a generous gift card," Brandy rambled. "And don't forget a crap-ton of books."

Two women with Boozy Book Bitches T-shirts passed them. One had her hands over her heart. "Cherry, you're not going to win."

"I can dream. I spent twenty-five dollars on tickets for it," Cherry replied.

"Yes, but that crazy Boba chick spent two-hundred—" the woman stopped talking when she spied Brandy and Sam's Boba Book Babe T-shirts.

Gina gasped and glanced at Brandy for confirmation. Brandy grinned and shrugged. "You know how she loves Jamison Blaine."

"Yeah, but two-hundred dollars is extreme." Gina guffawed.

"That girl loves her some Jamison." Sam chuckled. "She talks about him in her sleep."

"I've got to buy her some batteries." Brandy laughed. "I'm going to see LaShanda now."

"I'll go with you," Sam said.

"You can hold something." Brandy offered Sam the handle of the wagon.

"Great," Sam uttered.

"We'll meet you for lunch in conference room B. They'll have our box lunches available soon." Brandy waved as she took off at a steady clip. Sam didn't have an issue keeping up.

Conference room C had a police officer at the door. His eyes appeared glazed as the surrounding women talked about romance novels.

Gina spotted her sister in the corner. She had several long strips of raffle tickets in her grasp. She tore them into individual tickets as she faced a basket with a blanket and shifter books. Every once in a while, she glanced toward a cellophane-wrapped giveaway with a purple box base–the Jamison Blaine prize.

A green-haired lady placed a couple of tickets in the small paper bag for the Jamison Blaine giveaway, then a few in the next and the next, until she'd hit them all on the table. Cyndi returned to Jamison's basket and dropped a few tickets in.

"What are you doing?" Gina asked.

Cyndi jumped. "I've got a system."

Gina giggled and leaned in to read what Jamison offered. "Two VIP tickets to the Silenced in San Antonio event, handcrafted wine glasses, a bottle of cabernet, a fifty dollar gift card, swag, books, a free night stay at the hotel, and dinner with Jamison Blaine. One on one?" She glanced at Cyndi.

Her sister smiled as if she'd just discovered chocolate didn't have calories. "As far as I can tell." She rubbed her hands together. "I hope it's all night long."

"Brandy's going to buy you batteries." Gina poked her sister in the side.

Cyndi sighed. "You don't need batteries anymore. Those things are rechargeable."

Gina giggled again as they perused the items at the end of the room. A quilt caught Gina's eye. "It's such a cool idea." Gina pointed at the blanket depicting a bookshelf with different calico books.

Izzy happened to overhear the comment. "You should see the other quilts." She pointed to the other side of the room. "A local quilting book club made different quilts for the event and dropped off the raffle donation on Friday. If you don't win this year, they pledged to make more for next year's event."

"I'm glad they are having it next year," Cyndi said, dropping a few tickets into the bag.

"Usually, we raise thousands of dollars for charity, but this year..." Izzy frowned. "The murder have impacted sales."

"I'll get some tickets," Gina said, pulling out some cash.

"Awesome." Izzy smiled once more. "We'll announce the winners at the after-party tonight. You must be present to win. Bidding will go until the end. Despite the circumstances, we are trying to raise more than last year."

"Since I won a bet, Cyndi owes me ten tickets." Gina glanced at her sister with a wry grin.

Cyndi huffed, pulling out her wallet. "You better not enter the Jamison Blaine drawing."

Izzy practically glowed and skipped over to Barb. "We have a customer."

Gina took the ten tickets, shaking them over her head, then bought another fifty dollars worth. She spent a half-hour carefully studying the raffle goodies.

Gina dropped the ten tickets she'd won into the Jamison Blaine giveaway, then laughed when Cyndi covered them with her own.

"I've got a system," she repeated.

The sister's phones vibrated at the same time. Brandy had posted in the group chat. *At lunch.*

"We should meet them," Cyndi suggested.

Gina stuck her last ticket in the quilt bag, and they headed next door to the makeshift cafeteria. Sam raised her hand and waved them over.

"You get your choice of grilled chicken or ham and cheese," Brandy said, squirting mustard on her sandwich.

White boxes were stacked on two tables, each labeled with a selection. A hotel employee offered insight into the boxes' contents and pointed them in the direction of the drinks.

As the twins took a seat, Sam groused, "why couldn't they've had sweet tea?"

"You're sweet enough as you are," Gina said with a smirk.

"Don't you know it." Sam winked.

The sisters opened their lunches.

Gina caught them up on Redd's unexpected visit and her conversation with Duke as they ate.

"We knew it wasn't Ricky in that owl thing-a-ma-bob," Sam said, wadding up her sandwich wrap.

"Wrong tattoo," Brandy recalled. "It wasn't like Ricky. He's a weasel, but I think he'd prefer not to get his hands dirty. Literally."

"Does everyone have a tattoo except me?" Gina asked, staring at her naked wrists.

"I don't have one either," Sam said.

"You do too," Cyndi accused.

"Not where it counts." Sam blushed and sipped her drink.

The din in the room rose as groups of people filtered through. Some took a seat at the round tables, and others picked up their boxes and left.

"There's Molly," Brandy said, narrowing her eyes on the PA's exposed wrist. Dressed in a short black dress, thick tights, and black biker-style boots, she strode to the boxed lunches.

"She looks like crap," Cyndi observed. "What's up with the streaky black mascara and the dark circles?"

"Goth girls gone wild: the day after," Brandy said with a snort.

"The librarian edition," Gina added when Molly pushed her red glasses up her nose. "Does she have any tattoos?"

Molly shifted from one table to the other, seemingly indecisive. She opened one box and peered inside.

"Maybe. I can't remember, but I think I saw a tattoo yesterday when the models were signing books and taking pictures," Sam said, tapping her chin and glancing heavenward. "Let's check the photos."

"Great idea." Gina tapped her phone screen and saw a message from Austin. Poor Redd. It appeared Austin had his hands full. The models had to be a close-knit community. One loss, especially in such a brutal way, had to hit them hard. "Keep safe," she texted back.

"I saw Chad and Harrison leave the bar together yesterday," Tammy Shaver said to Barb as they waltzed by.

Cyndi whistled, indicating with her head toward Molly, Tammy, and Barb. The Boba Book Babes honed in on the conversation as the two hostesses gossiped.

"Ooooh. Who would have thought Chad Cummings was gay?" Barb said, shaking her head. "You don't think, Harrison..."

"What?" Tammy stopped next to Molly. "Do I think Harrison killed Rodney Stiff and Chad Cummings? PA and possible lover? Hmmm." Her forehead crinkled.

Molly's jaw dropped. She paled and stepped back a few feet from the women.

"Of course, it's possible, but I don't think he'd do it. He doesn't have the balls." Tammy picked a ham sandwich lunchbox.

"Plus, he'd make the perfect scapegoat." Barb took the chicken.

"You're right. It's too obvious," Tammy said, turning to Molly. She acknowledged Deidra's PA for the first time. "What do you think?"

Molly took a small pile of napkins and extra mayo packets. Her smile appeared forced. "About what?"

Tammy stared at Molly as if she'd grown an extra head. "Harrison Busch, of course."

Molly dropped the lunch boxes, napkins, and packets. She kneeled to pick up the mess. Barb stooped to help gather the scattered items.

"I got it," Molly muttered. "Thanks, though."

Barb shrugged, and she and Tammy walked away with their lunch.

"None of those ladies had wrist tattoos," Sam mentioned.

Molly closed her eyes and exhaled. When her lids popped open, her gaze skittered around the room nervously like a man with second thoughts about getting a vasectomy. She straightened, set her boxes on the table, then added the packets and napkins before fastening the containers. She smoothed the front of her dress, smearing something flesh-colored. After a second, she took the two boxes and practically ran out of the room.

"Molly's acting weird," Cyndi observed.

"I agree," Brandy said, unwrapping a chocolate chip cookie.

"Where did you get that?" Gina asked.

Brandy hummed, enjoying the sugary goodness. She pointed to a table in the far corner. Gina and Cyndi glanced at each other and stood in sync.

All kinds of cookies and brownies sprinkled with

powdered sugar filled trays. Gina selected a small brownie and an oatmeal raisin cookie, and Cyndi took two brownies.

Deidra Raines stormed into the room with her hands on her hips. Her petite frame vibrated with fury. Addie Werner hurried behind her, saying something in a low tone.

While the twins refilled their iced teas, they pretended not to eavesdrop. Gina nibbled on her brownie, thankful for the fudgy goodness and a sugar buzz.

"I don't know what happened," Addie said emphatically. "I swear."

"Molly is my PA, not yours," Deidra growled, whirling and poking a finger in Addie's chest.

"I didn't use her. I haven't seen her today. I promise." Addie raised her hands. "I have a college student doing some research for me. I swear."

"According to Molly, Addie did use her to research," Gina whispered to Cyndi.

Deidra glared, her brows forming a V. Her nose twitched. "I don't believe you."

The twins delayed as long as they could before returning to the table.

"If looks could kill," Cyndi whispered. The Bobas nodded.

"Deidra's angry, but is she mad enough to kill?" Gina asked.

"She's madder than a mule with a mouth full of bumblebees," Sam declared. "But she's a buck-five sopping wet."

"Yes, and she's short. She couldn't stick a dick sucker, or anything else, down Rodney's throat." Brandy leaned back and crossed her arms.

"She might have reached his belly button," Gina said with a smirk.

"Or his ass," Cyndi laughed. The rest joined in.

It felt good to belly laugh. It seemed like ages since genuine laughter had met her ears. She glanced around the room of readers and authors, all making the best out of a horrible situation.

Deidra tramped up to the table with the food and selected a box. She added a few condiment packs, then paraded from the room.

"Looks like she doesn't know Molly already got one for her," Brandy pointed out. "That's strange."

"Not if she hasn't seen or heard from her today." Cyndi met Gina's eyes.

"At least Molly is safe. Her phone is probably dead." Sam rose and gathered the table trash.

"Let's hope it's the only thing." Cyndi glanced at her phone. "Only five more hours until the party."

Brandy fluttered her eyelashes. "Jamison, my love."

Cyndi nudged Brandy. "Your turn is coming."

"All my turns cum." Brandy laughed.

"Seriously, we've got to figure this out, y'all." Sam stood with her hands on her hips.

The evening before Rodney's death, Deidra had glared at him and even got Barb upset. "Remember Deidra when we arrived?"

"Yes! She was as red as a sunburnt habanero." Sam glanced toward the exit.

"Would Molly do her bidding?" Cyndi asked, glancing at her sister.

"She's her personal assistant, not a hitman," Gina retorted.

"Everyone is a suspect until proven innocent," Brandy announced.

Chapter 14

Austin

I looked over my shoulder and heard crying.

Damn it. For such a giant of a man, no one would ever believe Redd Herrington could be a big baby.

Still slightly frustrated that every chance Gina and I had time alone, someone or something squashed our attempts to be intimate.

After snagging the leftover bottle of wine on the table, I grabbed a plastic cup from the bathroom and poured Redd a full cup. "Drink. You need it."

Redd wiped his red-rimmed eyes and accepted the cup. He chugged the wine in one large gulp and handed it back to me. "Thanks," he choked out.

Once I got rid of the empty bottle and cup, I sat in the chair adjacent to the bed, where Redd took up the space.

"Now tell me, why are you so upset?"

"Chad."

"What about Chad?" I could have added "he's dead," but that would only add fuel to his emotional fire.

"I... I...," Redd scrubbed both hands over his face. "I liked him, you know?"

"Yeah. He was a good guy. I liked him too—"

"No, Austin. I *really liked* him."

I stared at my friend, finally realizing the enormity of what Redd was admitting to me. That was huge. He was a straight man, confessing his feelings for a dead guy.

"Redd, I didn't know you—"

"I'm not. Not really." He stood and started pacing. "I like girls—always have. But in the last year, hanging with Chad, working out, and going to dinner and movies, my feelings slowly changed. I didn't see our friendship shift until we got here and we... you know... made love." Redd dropped back onto the bed. "I didn't get a chance to tell him how I truly felt."

What could I say to him? And the explicit knowledge that they had sex blew my mind.

"Redd, listen to me. You can't kick yourself for that. No one knew this shit was going to happen. Hell, I thought Chad was hooking up with Harrison."

"What?" His head snapped up, eyes wide, and mouth gaped open. "He told me he was single."

Oh shit. I did it now. "Redd, I assumed—I could be wrong."

"I want to talk to that little asshole boyfriend stealer," he growled and stood, his hands fisted at his side. "Where is he?"

"You need to calm down, Redd."

He leaned in, inches from my face. "Austin, where is that son-of-a-bitch?"

I shook my head and slowly stood. "I don't know."

"He has to be down by the event." Redd stalked to the door, then stopped before opening it. "Are you coming?"

"How about this? Let's see if he's in his room," I said, hoping to cool the man's temper by misdirecting him to the floor above us. I had seen Redd mad before but never like this. If he got his hands on Harrison, he would be in a world of hurt, and I alone wouldn't be able to stop Redd from pummeling the small man.

We got to the elevator, but it took too long. So, I decided to take the stairs. Besides, it was good for Redd to work off the angry adrenaline coursing through his veins.

"I thought he was on your floor," he said, taking each step with a hard clomp of his boots.

"I heard he moved," I lied.

He pushed the door open, and we found ourselves at the far end of the hallway. Female voices echoed off the walls as we headed toward the middle, where the elevators were.

Chad and Rod Stiff's names bounced back to us. Redd's stalking shifted to hulking as he strode toward the two women talking about the murders and how they would do it if they were the killers.

"Redd," I called out the warning.

"What do you know about Chad?" Redd growled in the women's faces.

The closer I got to the duo, I recognized the authors. The short blonde was Keeley Wetstone, author of young adult romance. And the tall redhead was BJ Dickson, whose books consisted of BDSM and erotica.

"Step back, buster." BJ had her hand in Redd's face. "I know how to use my foot and it's about to kick your ass."

"Redd, back up. Give the ladies space," I insisted with a hand on his shoulder.

Redd did, but not before he spat out, "Where is that weasel, Harrison?"

"I don't know. I haven't seen him," Keeley admitted with a huff. "Have you seen him, Bev?"

BJ shook her head. "I haven't seen him. Now you can go beat off."

"Come on. I remembered I have to meet Gina and the girls in the lobby. Maybe they saw Harrison down there." I hated to tell Redd more lies, but the way he was acting, if I told him the truth, he would tear this hotel apart looking for the man.

Redd's shoulders slumped. "Okay." The defeat and heartbreak in his ice-blue eyes had me yearning to be with Gina.

I couldn't imagine anyone, especially someone like Redd, who found the love of his life, only to lose him to a murderer. If I'd lost Gina, there was nothing on this earth that would make me happy again.

The elevator ride was quiet, except for a few sniffles from Redd. The second the door opened to the main floor, chaos ensued, with loud shouts coming from the lobby.

Redd and I looked at each other before we rushed out of the elevator to investigate what the hell was going on.

There, three of the Boozy Book Bitches were standing off with two of the event coordinators.

Spotting Gina across the lobby, my heart skipped at the wide smile on her beautiful face. She waved us over, where the girls were watching the verbal smackdown.

"What's going on?" I asked, my attention on the dispute.

"How about a kiss first?" Gina said as she tiptoed and kissed me. It was chaste, but it was enough for now.

"How about saving that crap for your room," Cyndi doled out.

"Yeah, stop. Some people don't want to see that." Redd turned to the girls. "Did you see Harrison?" he snapped.

I glared at my friend. I know he's upset about Chad, but he had no right to talk to the Babes that way. "Redd."

"Sorry," he muttered, his eyes shifted to the two shouting women.

"So, what's going on?" I said lazily, with a smile only for Gina.

"Tammy and Barb overheard Jacki and another Boozy Book Bitch talking about how Rod had stolen a lot of the ideas for his stories. I guess he had also plagiarized several authors, and there are lawsuits confirming it."

Sam squeezed between Redd and me, slurping on a straw. "This is exciting to watch."

"You are wrong about Ricky. He is not the killer. He wouldn't even harm a fly," Jacki shouted out, red-faced, and a bit of spital sprayed from her mouth.

"Then why did he get hauled away by the cops? He was the one who posted on his Facebook and blog about the lies. Rodney Stiff would never steal other people's ideas. Ricky had to have killed him, and the model too," Barb countered with a righteous smirk, like she knew the truth. Tammy nodded emphatically, agreeing with her friend, while Izzy shook her head but smiled in her usual way.

"Whoa," Cyndi said from beside Gina. "I can't believe she thinks Ricky is the killer."

"He's the killer, Jacki. So, I suggest since you're the president of that blog group, take down those falsehoods, or you're going to have problems," Barb continued on her rant.

"You can kiss my ass. I approved that post, and it will stay up because it's the truth. And you better take that back about Ricky." Jacki growled out. All the Boozy Book Bitches stood behind her like sentinels.

Strength in numbers, I guess.

"I think it's best we step back. Jacki looks like she's about to combust," Brandy chuckled as she slurped boba balls through her straw.

"Hey."

We all turned and spotted Ricky, tired and pale, walking toward the group of women.

The Bitches surrounded him like a cocoon of friendship. Jacki spun back around, her middle finger in the air, to Barb and Tammy. "I told you, Raggedy Anns, Ricky was innocent."

"Whatever," Barb huffed out. "His blog still sucks."

"Are you hungry?" Gina asked, her warm hand in mine.

"Famished," I said with a rub on my growling belly.

She then tugged me by the hand toward the conference room.

Chapter 15

Gina

Hotel security arrived and the Peoria PD descended on the crowd. Readers and authors melted away.

Gina continued tugging on Austin's hand. He acquiesced, and she led him around the hubbub to the small conference room with the lunches.

Redd followed Gina and the group, his bloodshot eyes roaming every person. He shuffled along like a sad postal worker, one comment away from going postal.

A small crowd filtered into the makeshift lunch room.

"You have a choice of sandwich," Gina informed, pointing toward the table. "I can get you both a drink. Tea, lemonade, or water?"

"Water for me. Thanks," Austin said with a soft smile.

"Is there any booze?" Redd chimed in a low growl.

"No." Cyndi eyed the model.

"Water," he muttered.

Gina and Cyndi moseyed to the beverage table and waited in line to get the men's drinks.

Cyndi leaned in. "They're all riled up now." The tables

were filled, and the noise level rose as women whispered theories and engaged in animated conversations about the hostility between Tammy, Barb, and Jacki, Ricky's innocence, and the possible truth behind Rod Stiff's plagiarizing.

"Like bees who don't know whether to swarm or get to work." Gina glanced around the room.

"You know it. What's up with Redd?" Cyndi stared at the man sitting, bent over the table, head in his hands. Sam tried to engage him in conversation, but Redd shook his head. Austin shrugged apologetically before taking a bite of his sandwich.

"I don't know. He was upset earlier. Now he seems pissed and depressed."

"Why don't you find out?" Cyndi poked her sister in the side. "Text Austin."

"Oh. Good idea." Gina hastily texted a question as they stepped to the front of the line. Gina glanced over at Austin as she held a plastic cup for Cyndi to fill. Austin tapped his screen, frowned, and looked up. He met her gaze and slowly shook his head. Then his eyes dropped to the phone, and he typed a reply, *Later.*

"Now's not the time to talk. I'm sure we'll find out soon enough," Gina said as three women approached Austin and Redd's table. They tried to engage the models in conversation. Redd's face turned more crimson with each passing second. Austin stood with a smile. He signed a book and posed for a picture while Redd, elbows on the table, buried his face in his hands again.

"Maybe he was going to pose with Chad for a Rodney Stiff cover?" Cyndi surmised.

Gina shivered, remembering Chad's soulless eyes. She was going to have nightmares about his lifeless body pinning her. Every minute spent with Austin helped her forget.

"Maybe he broke up with his girlfriend? Or he probably isn't getting paid for the weekend, too, since he was here for Rodney Stiff," Gina added.

"Or all of the above," her sister said as she waded through the throng, clearing the way for Gina to follow in her wake.

They set the beverages down. Austin pulled out the empty seat next to him and offered it to Gina. She slunk into it with a soft sigh.

Anxiety, muted excitement, and confusion hung low and thick in the room, covering the occupants like a wet blanket. The din rose as the room filled. The numbing noise made it easy to retreat inward and flip on observation mode.

Tammy, Izzy, Barb, and a few volunteers sat with paperwork splayed on a circular table. Joy oozed out of Izzy, and her hands swished as she talked like she conducted the world's largest orchestra. Barb blinked occasionally but otherwise appeared pale and withdrawn. With arms pulled tight over her chest, Tammy leered at Gina.

Cyndi scooted closer. "Tammy doesn't like you very much."

Gina sighed, too tired to care.

"That's an understatement." Brandy matched Tammy's glare and crossed arms but tipped her head, adding her nose in the air.

Redd wiped his eyes with the back of his hand and glanced over his untouched lunch at the event coordinators. He offered, "She's been after Austin since the DC event."

Gina pressed her lips together. When she wasn't scowling, Tammy could be considered pretty. She had full lips, long dark hair and lashes, a creamy, clear complexion, and soulful eyes. She also had big bosoms—or bazookas, as Duke Wain would say. Some men are boob guys, and she'd amply fulfill those interests. She had a bold personality and when she wanted something, she probably pushed until she got it. Had Austin given into Tammy's wiles at a previous event, and was that why she'd become so territorial?

Gina turned her gaze to Austin, who still posed with varying readers. He smiled, hugged, chatted, and eased the women's worries, helping them enjoy the remnants of the book event. Tammy Shaver didn't seem his type...

"Gina, why are you frowning?" Cyndi nudged her. "I'll bet you a million dollars Austin shut her down—"

"Quicker than Detective Dick downs donuts," Sam finished.

Gina nodded and laid her head on Cyndi's boney shoulder. Her eyes fluttered closed as she rested in her sister's hug.

"Some weekend, huh?" Cyndi lamented.

"You could say that," Sam agreed.

"It's not all been bad," Brandy said.

Gina's eyes snapped open. Everyone at the table stared at Brandy.

She swirled her boba tea. After a beat of silence, she glanced up. Her cheeks flared crimson. "What? It's true. Gina found Austin again, and I met..." She waved her hand. "Authors. Got my pre-orders too."

Gina straightened with a sigh. No denying how fate had rolled her book cover boyfriend and high school crush into a sexy, sweet, protective man and dropped him into her lap. Although, so far, fate had kept him out of her bed. She sighed again.

Brandy asked Redd about his modeling origin story.

Her questions about his first modeling gig loosened his mouth and lessened his pained expression.

"I stood by the fountain, and the photographer wanted me to pose. He got frustrated with me and hopped on the edge. You'll never guess what happened." Redd's lips hinted at a grin.

"Did you push him in?" Brandy asked.

"No. I didn't have to. He slipped and landed on his ass in the freezing water." Redd continued the story, and Gina glanced around.

Duke Wain burst into the room. His eyes were wearily traveling around the space, like he was looking for someone. He stopped mid-step when everyone turned to inspect him. He ran his fingers through his wispy hair and nodded. His wild gaze bounced over to Austin. Duke hesitantly started forward. He met Gina's eyes, and then his gaze fell on her man again. He picked up the pace.

Gina stood and rushed to Austin's side. She touched his arm and pointed to Duke.

"Hey, babe," Austin grinned at Gina. Her insides melted, and she kept from leaning against him. He turned to a couple of women taking a photo with him. "If you'll excuse me, ladies."

Austin took Gina's hand. "I have a bad feeling about Duke," she said for his ears only.

Austin studied the older man with a keen eye. Breathless, he stopped beside them.

"Duke, what's going on?" Austin asked.

"It's about Harrison Busch."

Redd jumped to his feet and hovered behind Gina. "What about him?"

Duke's gaze scrubbed the room's occupants again before snapping back to Redd. "I can't find him anywhere."

"Why do you want him?" Redd asked, pushing past Gina.

Austin put his arm around her and tucked her against him. He glared at the back of Redd. The man hadn't moved from his spot at the table until now.

Brandy, Sam, and Cyndi joined the huddle around the older man.

Duke leaned forward. "Can I trust you?" He studied their faces. Cyndi nodded.

Brandy reached for Duke's hand and patted it. "Sure you can, buddy. We've got you."

Duke glanced at Brandy's hand. A loud sigh escaped. He squared his shoulders and raised his head, offering a stiff nod. "Thank you."

"What's this about, Duke?" Gina asked, squeezing tighter into Austin's solid body.

Narrow-eyed, he rotated his gaze outside the circle of the small group. "Not here." Duke lowered his voice. "There's too much at stake to talk here. We need to go someplace private. Follow me." He motioned for the group to follow.

"What's going on?" Redd finally chimed in, his hulking form hovered near Cyndi.

"We're following Duke somewhere to have privacy," Austin explained.

Duke took the lead with Brandy and Sam shadowed closely by Redd. Once more Cyndi traipsed in front of Gina, adding a sense of comfort with her "get out of my way bitch" expression, especially when they passed the glowering Tammy.

The western author led the group through the throng toward the exit. Austin kept a hand on Gina's lower back.

Steady and warm, she couldn't help the smile that manifested. His touch made her feel valued and protected.

In the lobby, Tanya Fitzpatrick interviewed Keeley Wetstone. The YA author held her newest release to her chest as the reporter ignored the book and asked about the murders.

Duke paused when they mentioned Harrison's name.

A fleeting glance in the Boba Book Babes' direction had Tanya smiling. New audience, new fodder.

"Now, Harrison Busch is missing. Do you know Rodney Stiff's PA well?" Tanya asked Keeley, holding the mic under her nose.

Cross-eyed, Keeley gaped at the red tipped mic. Her jaw hung open, but nothing came out.

"For an author you don't use many words," Tanya mumbled as she rolled her eyes. "Let's try this again. About Stiff's PA. Did you know him?"

Keeley's mouth snapped shut. She squared her shoulders and glared at the reporter. "Not really. I saw him here and there. Author events. Signings. We weren't friends if that's what you want to know. As far as I knew, he was a good PA. He did what he needed to help Rod and maybe more." Her eyes shifted around the lobby.

"Go on," Tanya prompted.

"There were rumors that Rod and Harrison were lovers."

"Bullshit," Duke spat softly.

Keeley hurried to add, "But there were rumors Rod had slept with most authors and models. Men and women. I don't know what to believe anymore." She rubbed her face.

"Thank you for your time." Tanya turned to face the cameraman. "That was young adult author Keeley Wetstone..."

"Is it true about Rod and Harrison, Duke?" Gina asked.

"Don't listen to that nonsense." Duke turned his back to the newshound and strode toward the elevator bay. He pushed the up arrow, and they silently waited. His crimson face matched Redd's.

The bell pinged. With a whoosh, the doors opened. Jacki and her Boozy Book Bitch lackeys, Cherry and Mary Sue, exited, leaving a wake of strong rose perfume mixed with stale cigarette smoke.

Cyndi waved her hand in front of her nose while grimacing.

Sam mumbled, "You can't cover the smell of shit with flowers."

Brandy took a large draught of air and held her breath as she stepped into the empty elevator. The girls lined the back wall. Austin hugged Gina to his chest. The rhythm of his heart relaxed her, and she wrapped her arms around his waist. Why couldn't she take him aside and stay in his arms forever?

Oh yeah. A murderer or two was on the loose. *And Harrison is MIA.*

Duke pushed the button. Only the drone of the machinery and the group's breathing sounded as they moved. Stone-faced, Redd stared at the seam where the doors met. The lift jerked to a stop on the seventh floor.

They filed out. Duke led them to his room. He glanced both ways before unlocking the door. Once inside, he crumbled into a seat with his head in his hands, one knee bobbing.

Brandy took a seat on the edge of the made bed closest to Duke as if ready for whatever he had to say.

Redd's patience wore thin, and he began to pace. Sam pulled the other seat out and lowered herself.

Housekeeping had yet to make the other bed, and extra pillows dotted the floor. An emerald-green sequined vest and bow tie laid on the made bed, presumably for the Oz-themed after-party.

"Well?" Redd said with hands on his hips.

Duke lifted his face, his eyes shining with unspent tears. "Duke Wain is my author name." he cleared his throat. "My real name is Bernard—"

"What about Harrison?" Redd demanded.

Austin stepped between Redd and Duke. "Let him speak, Redd. He brought us here in confidence."

With a frown, Redd shoved his hands into his pockets. He clamped his mouth shut.

"Go on, Bernard," Austin said.

"I'm Bernard Busch. Harrison is my son. At events, I prefer to go by my pseudonym."

Gina met Cyndi's wide eyes.

"Do you know where he is?" Gina asked, rubbing her chin.

Duke appeared to shrink into the chair. He scrubbed his face with both hands. "No. After the hubbub last night, I called him, but he didn't answer. Then I looked for his location on my phone. He was still in the building, but I don't know where."

"He didn't come to you?" Austin asked.

Duke shook his head. "I'd hoped he would, but..."

"Why tell us?" Brandy asked.

He met Gina's gaze. "You guys were here when everything went down. You know he's innocent. I need your help to find him."

Gina glanced at Austin. They'd heard the fight and had seen the note and the owl lady, but they couldn't rule Harrison out as the murderer.

Cyndi jumped up. "We can go floor to floor and use your phone to find him."

Bernard shook his head again. "His phone is off or dead. It goes straight to voicemail."

"So, he didn't leave like the police believe," Redd said.

"Or, his phone didn't," Sam offered.

"Are you sure you didn't see where he was?" Redd asked, pacing.

"The dot was here." Duke pointed to the floor. "Like he was in my room, but he wasn't."

"He could have been in a room directly under or over you," Austin suggested.

Redd growled, fists clutching his hair. He spun and stalked up to Duke. "Where is he? You are hiding him." A vein throbbed on his forehead, and his jaw tensed.

Duke rose to his feet, tears threatening to spill. He poked Redd in the chest. "If I knew where my son was, I wouldn't have asked you to help me find him."

"You're covering for him." The beefy model closed the space and towered over the man.

"For what?"

"He killed the man I love, and you are helping him get away with it," Redd spat.

"You loved Rodney Stiff?" Brandy asked, frowning. Sam's mouth hung open.

"No, of course not, you idiots. Who could love that asshole?" Redd growled out, rubbing his temples.

"Ahh. Chad," Cyndi said softly. Redd's head dropped, and he covered his face with his hands and started crying again.

Gina grasped onto Austin's arm and met his eyes. "But Chad and Harrison were..."

Chapter 16

Austin

I lay a finger on Gina's lips before she belted out the rest of her question.

Redd bounced to his feet and stalked toward Gina. "There is no Chad and Harrison. It is Chad and me... was..." His angry demeanor deflated.

I pulled her behind me and faced off with Redd. "Keep your distance from my girl."

"But she said—"

"I know what she said. I need you to calm your ass down, or we're going rounds. Get me?" I warned. Gina's fingers fisted the back of my shirt, like she was trying to hold me back from pummeling my friend.

Redd nodded. His shoulder slumped slightly and more tears slid down his ruddy cheeks.

"What about my son, dammit?" Duke raked his fingers through his thinning hair. "I'm really worried. Something must have happened to him. I know it."

"What about Chad? Who killed him?" Redd said as he rubbed at his watery eyes.

"I'm sorry, son. I have no clue who killed your person, but here," Duke passed him a full bottle of Jack, "this always works for me when I'm down."

Redd glanced at the bottle and then at me. He swiped the liquor out of the author's hands and stormed out.

The air suddenly lightened a bit with Redd's absence.

"Okay, Duke. What do you want us to do? We don't have a clue where Harrison is," Brandy said as she sat on the end of the bed.

"Maybe this will help." Duke went into the cabinet housing the small safe, an ironing board, and an extra pillow.

We all looked perplexed as Duke took out a laptop.

"It's your laptop," Sam said drolly.

"It's more than a laptop—and it's not mine," Duke countered with a frown and tapped the lid. "And what's inside it is important."

"And that is?" I took a step to get a better look at the computer, but Duke clutched it to his chest.

"Secrets." The old man's word was barely audible.

"What secrets?" Cyndi added. She, too, stood to get a better look at the computer.

It was Gina, with her calm demeanor, who eased the rising tension radiating from Duke. "Are you saying that laptop has clues to who killed Rod Stiff and Chad?"

"No, girly. What I'm saying is that this is Rodney Stiff's secret. You see, Harrison told me a few weeks ago that he was doing some work for Jamison Blaine."

Cyndi's eyes widened.

"Calm down, Cyn," Gina insisted. "Go on, Duke."

"Well, I don't know what my son was doing, but I overheard a phone conversation he had with someone and mentioned *plagiarizing*."

"Wait?" Cyndi raised her hand. "Are you telling us Harrison is working with Jamison Blaine—" Brandy began to chuckle but was quickly cut short when Gina's sister gave her devil eyes. "As I was saying. You think Harrison has proof Rodney Stiff was plagiarizing his stories?"

"Possibly." Duke dropped back into the chair and placed the laptop on the small table. "Harrison doesn't know I have it."

"I don't understand. You just said..." Gina took the other chair and stared at the laptop.

Duke shook his head. "I took it right after Stiff was murdered. Harrison doesn't know I grabbed it, and I haven't had the chance to tell him."

"Why did you take it if you knew your son needed it?" I asked. I flanked Gina's back and placed a hand on her shoulder. There was heat in her beautiful brown eyes, which perked up my interest.

"Harrison hated Rodney. He took all my son's ideas and used them for his stories. The last book that came out finally nailed that coffin, so to speak."

"That still doesn't explain why you took the laptop," Sam said.

"To protect my son. I don't know what exactly is in this laptop, but I'll protect it if it will save Harrison from taking the fall for those murders." He let out an exhausted breath and rubbed his eyes. "I need to find my son. But I'm one person, and I haven't slept much since I got here."

"We'll help, right ladies?" Brandy said, then glanced at me. "Austin will help too."

"I will," I admitted.

"How's this," Gina started. "You hold on to the computer, go get some sleep, and we'll go ask around about

Harrison. We can meet up at four down by the main lobby. Sounds good?"

Duke wiped his wet eyes and hushed out a breath. "Okay."

"Let's go, girls." Gina corralled her friends and sister toward the door, while our fingers laced tight together.

"One more thing," Duke called out. "Harrison also mentioned in that phone call about an author assistant who was angry at Rodney and him. I don't know the name, but she wanted revenge from the sounds of it. So be careful."

"I'll make sure nothing happens to them, Duke." I then closed the door.

"Poor guy," Sam uttered to Brandy.

"Maybe he shouldn't have given Redd the bottle of Jack. Duke looks like he needs it just as much," Brandy added.

"Shiitake mushrooms. This weekend is turning into a cluster. Two murders and several suspects, but no concrete evidence to who killed Rod and Chad."

The five of us headed to the main lobby, where people were loitering around the news reporter taking interviews.

"People will do anything for five minutes of fame," Gina said as Tammy talked animatedly to the reporter.

"Oh, and here's one of our gorgeous cover models." Tammy scrambled over to me and tugged at my free arm.

The cameraman shuffled over, along with the reporter, and stuck the microphone in my face. "What is your name?

I glanced at Gina, who was elbowed out of the way by Tammy. "This is Austin Blackmoor. He's on over fifty book covers. Isn't he beautiful?" She gushed.

I wanted to get away from this handsy woman, but her grip on my bicep wouldn't allow me to step back and out of the limelight.

"What made you decide to model?" the reporter asked with a brilliant fake-white smile.

"That's a brilliant question, Tanya. I always wanted to know more about this cutie." Tammy batted her fake eyelashes, which reminded me of deformed spider legs.

I was absolutely miserable. Tammy slathered up next to me while Gina, the woman I wanted, sent imaginary ice picks at Tammy's face. I shook Tammy's hands off my arm and strode over to Gina, whose eyes went from hard to shocked and moony.

The reporter followed me. "Wait. Please answer the question, Mr. Blackmoor."

"The reason why, um," I turned to the reporter. "I got into modeling because I needed the cash."

"That's interesting." Tanya's gaze quickly perused my body and then snapped back to my face. She turned to Gina. "And who are you?"

Before Gina could respond, I jumped in and rattled out, "She's my girlfriend."

Gina's fingers tighten around my wrist. I wasn't sure if it was a good or bad thing telling the world, or the Peoria area, that Gina was my girlfriend. But I didn't care. She was mine back then and now.

Tammy huffed, which made Gina smile.

"Well, Austin, as a model in this industry, can you tell me how you feel about these murders? Who do you think did it? Were there rivals bent on revenge? Tell me, what did the bodies look like?"

Before I got a word out, Officer Cox appeared out of nowhere. "The investigation is ongoing, and we will let you know if there are more details on the cases. Thank you."

"Well, thank you for that," Tanya said in a snoot. She

turned and asked Barb and Tammy about the charity raffle instead.

"I'm glad you asked, Tanya. The after-party dinner is on, and the theme is Wizard of Oz. You can still buy tickets for the raffle. All proceeds go to a good cause–"

Gina squeezed my hand and whispered, "So, I'm your girlfriend?"

I tilted my head and kissed the tip of her nose. "Yes, you are my girl."

"Then we need to consummate this relationship." The twinkle in her eyes was so damn adorable.

"How do we break away?"

"I'm going to check out the baskets again and ask around if anyone has seen Harrison," Cyndi said, then winked at her sister.

A princess wave from Deidra pulled my attention from the snickering Babes. She marched past us toward the bar.

"Oh, my effing God. Come here." Breathing heavily, Brandy appeared out of nowhere.

"Where the heck did you go?" Sam's fisted hands were on her hips.

"Where did you come from?" Cyndi eyed her friend.

"I went to the bathroom and guess what I saw on Deidra Raines?" Brandy leaned in and waved them even closer.

"What?" all three girls asked in unison. *Kinda Freaky.*

"She had a tattoo on the same place as Chad's killer. And–" She paused for dramatics.

"Geez, just tell us." Cyndi scowled with impatience.

Brandy waved her off. "She had her newsletter sign up with her, and 'Kill RS' was written all over it."

Officer Cox popped her head next to Brandy like a ninja, surprising the group. She ordered Brandy to repeat what she said. Then, the cop got on her radio and called for backup.

Detective Burns was not far behind her when they apprehended the belligerent woman, who was talking to a couple of other authors in the bar.

"I told you I didn't kill that asshole." Deidra's screams echoed off the walls of the lounge area. She fought them like a wild cat, kicking and swiping her fingernails at Officer Cox.

"We didn't say you killed Mr. Stiff. We're talking about Mr. Chad Cummings," Burns ruefully explained before he grabbed her wrist and twisted it behind her back. Then he read her the Miranda Rights as one of the uniformed officers pulled out handcuffs and quickly slapped them on Deidra's wrists.

"I want my lawyer. I'm going to sue you all for wrongful arrest." Spittle sprayed out with each word.

"Yeah, yeah. You can make your one call when we get to the station," Cox stated, hauling the author away.

"Well, I didn't see that coming," Sam said, shaking her head.

"Me either," Cyndi added while the crazed author refused to get into the squad car.

"It's a shame," Brandy muttered.

"What's a shame? Cyndi asked.

"I loved her writing—ooh, do you think she could write a kinky prison romance?"

Everyone groaned, including me.

"I think I had enough fun for a bit." Gina let out a mock yawn. "I think I'm going to take a nap."

Cyndi waved her off. "You and your lover can go take your nap. We three are going to ask about Harrison and maybe buy more raffle tickets."

I opened my mouth to refute Cyndi's claim, but with a tug on my arm, I graciously followed behind Gina, mesmerized by the sway of her ass.

Thankfully, we were in the elevator alone.

She pressed the number for my floor, and a shot of lust ignited my blood, knowing what was about to happen.

"Nice ploy," I say with a smile.

"Why, thank you." Gina batted her lashes and stepped nearer until our chests were pressed close. "Seriously, I know it might be too fast, but I don't want to wait until you wine and dine me, Philly. We've known each other for a long time, and we're two adults—"

I didn't let her finish the sentence before I bent in and took her mouth like I owned it. We kissed like two love-starved virgins.

We barely made it to my room before our clothing peeled off.

"Oh, Gina," I moaned as our bodies melded into the mattress. "You feel so good."

"Less talking, more kissing and touching."

Her demands rocked my world and my shaft. As her hands mapped out my back, I was desperate to taste her. I started down her chin, along her neck, kissing her collarbone.

Her breasts were more than bountiful, but I was willing to take the time and explore.

As I sucked the tight pink bud into my mouth, there was a spastic knocking at my damn door.

"What the heck? Not again." Gina cried.

"Don't move," I ordered and ran to the door. I looked through the peephole and was taken aback by who was standing there.

"Who is it?" Gina whispered.

I turn to look at my beautiful person, all lust drunk and frustrated. "Molly. Deidra's PA. And she's crying."

"Crap." Gina got up and tossed my clothes to me. "Get dressed."

I quickly slid my legs into the jeans while Gina dragged her shirt over her delectable body.

Once we were presentable, I opened the door.

"Oh, Austin. I'm glad you're here." She stormed into the room, a purple pen in her grip and wrapped herself around me.

I stood in stunned silence. Molly had never been touchy like that before. I looked at Gina, who was more than upset by the situation. She kept staring at the pen in Molly's hand.

"Gina," I called out, wanting her help.

She snapped out of whatever daze and promptly walked over, pulling me out of Molly's arms. "Why are you here?" she demanded.

"Oh, I didn't see you." Molly turned to Austin and pouted. "I'm sorry. I didn't know you had company."

"What's wrong? Why are you crying?" I asked while trying to sound put out. I hardly knew Molly, only seeing her from time to time at book events. But never once did I see her so distraught.

"I just heard about Deidra, and I'm so upset," Molly said with another bout of tears.

"We all saw her getting handcuffed," Gina admitted, her features softened.

"Well, I'm not surprised. She was an angry woman. I should have told the police about how she hated Rodney, and she was jealous of Chad sleeping with Harrison and a bunch of other people."

"So, you think Deidra killed both men?" I asked, shocked at her admission.

"I know more than people think. And I have proof," Molly said with conviction.

Gina's shocked eyes locked onto mine, and I knew there would be no sexy time for us right now.

Chapter 17

Gina

Gina huffed as she glared at Molly. *So much for getting up close and personal with the sexiest man on the planet.* She balled her fists and closed her eyes. She couldn't blame Molly that the weekend had gone to hell in a book basket. It was the murderer's fault.

Her eyes snapped open, and Gina studied Molly anew. Her exasperated expression, mousy hair, and flouncy dress gave Molly an air of innocence. But her black thick-soled biker boots boosted her height, and the red-framed glasses added to the librarian look, like a goth book nerd.

She twirled the author's pen on her knee. Could she be the murderer?

Everyone is a suspect until proven innocent. Brandy's words echoed in Gina's mind.

After all, Molly had pawned off the dick suckers to the models. Austin shoved his basket toward her when he'd gone to hug Gina at their reunion.

What were the odds Gina would bump into Austin at the event?

Fate was a fickle bitch. She'd given Gina a second chance at her first love. And her heart soared at what the future could hold, especially with Austin at her side.

But the world had been robbed of Rodney Stiff and his brilliance. How many readers depended on his stories to escape reality? Gina's brow furrowed. What if Rod's stories weren't really his, as Duke suggested? What if her favorite author turned out to be a thief? The laptop would reveal the truth. She shook her head, rubbing her temples.

First things first. Put the criminal behind bars so they couldn't hurt anyone else.

"Molly," Gina sat on the bed and patted beside her. "Take a deep breath."

Molly's chest expanded as she inhaled. She took off her red frames and wiped her eyes as she sat beside Gina. After smoothing the skirt of her black dress, she sighed.

"I don't know what you have on Deidra, but you should tell Detective Burns or Officer Cox." Austin got Molly a glass of water and handed it to her.

"I know." Molly sniffed and stuck the pen in her pocket. She sipped and nodded. "Did you know Rodney stole from other authors?" Her gaze darted from Austin's to Gina's, then landed in her lap.

Gina met Austin's eyes. She swallowed, unable to betray Duke's confidence.

Austin rubbed his face. "I've heard rumors from other authors or PAs." He began slowly pacing.

"Oh?" Molly raised her face and sniffled. Her narrowed gaze followed Austin's movement. "What rumors?"

Austin waved his hand. "Just rumors."

"I bet Harrison Busch would know," Gina suggested, gauging Molly's reaction.

Molly gasped as her eyebrows flew skyward. She chewed her lower lip.

Gina reached for Austin's hand, stopping him from pacing.

He smiled at her. "Harrison probably would know something. I guess we should make an effort to find him." He hauled Gina to her feet.

"What's that going to accomplish? He's already talked to the police," Molly groused.

"Do you think it's true Rodney plagiarized? And why would he do it?" Gina asked, wrapping her arms around Austin's waist possessively.

Molly shrugged. "He was too busy or lazy and didn't want to work. Who knows? Rod didn't like to do his own research. That much I know," she spat, rising.

Austin glanced at his watch. "It's almost time to meet your sister and friends."

"Already?" Gina pouted, then sighed.

"I–I guess I should head out. I need to go to my room and check on..." Molly frowned and stomped toward the door. "I mean, get the evidence." She glanced through the peephole, then turned around, chugging what was left of her water.

"If you see Harrison, tell him the police want to talk to him again," Austin said. His gaze honed in on Molly's face.

She laughed without humor.. "If I see Harrison, I'll run the other direction. He's probably the mastermind."

"What makes you think that?" Gina and Austin shared a look. She pictured the raging scrawny man when he confronted the Boozy Book Bitches and the violent fight with Chad.

"Harrison had access to all of Rodney's writing. I know he snooped around, asking specific questions to Deidra about her work in progress. Research type questions." Her lids narrowed, and anger flashed in her eyes. She pressed her lips into a line.

Austin fished in his back pocket and pulled out a business card. "Contact Officer Cox. She'll listen to you."

Gina nodded. "She might come across as bossy, but she'll give you a fair shake."

Molly stared at the little paper as if it would burn her. She finally acquiesced and slipped it into her dress pocket.

The blousy material of Molly's dress appeared soft in juxtaposition of her stiff back and locked jaw.

Gina's phone chimed, and she glanced at the screen. Brandy and the girls hadn't found Harrison in the lobby, bar, or raffle room. Although Gina was certain Cyndi probably found more tickets.

"The Boba Book Babes are in the lobby." Gina noticed the time. It hadn't been almost time to meet the girls. She pointed to the numbers on the screen. With his back to Molly, Austin wiggled his brows.

The temperature of the room escalated. The butterflies in her stomach took flight as she recalled the press of his erection against her skin. He'd wanted to get rid of Molly so they could finish what they started. A shiver of desire trailed to her core.

It was time for Molly to go.

Molly checked out the peephole again. With a hint of a smirk, she waved. "Thanks for the water." She opened the door a crack.

"I'm sure Officer Cox will be happy to see you," Austin said.

"Yeah. Sure. Whatever." Molly slipped out the barely open door and closed it in Gina and Austin's face.

"What was that?" Gina asked.

"She's weird." Austin faced Gina, resting his hands on her shoulders.

"That's the understatement of the year..." Her voice trailed off as his lusty gaze bored into her. With her hands on his chest, she felt his wildly beating heart. Heat radiated off his body, calling her like a siren.

"We've got a few minutes," he whispered, lowering his lips to hers.

"Not enough," Gina growled through the kiss. She pulled out his shirt, sliding her hands over his skin to his back.

Austin chuckled and pressed her against the wall. His hands skimmed her sides as he deepened the kiss. The coolness against her back was a contrast to his hot body.

Voices, door closings, and footsteps echoed in from the other side of the door. Austin's lavished kisses muted everything, leaving her breathless. Her hands dipped into his jeans, groping his perfect rear. He groaned and broke the kiss.

His sultry whiskey-brown eyes tenderly studied her, and her heart hitched. He caressed her cheek, and she pressed into his gentle touch. "I don't have time to love you like you deserve," he said with seriousness.

"How much time do you need?" The question spurted out unfiltered, and her face heated.

He lowered until he was eye to eye with her, and breathed, "A lifetime."

Tears welled in her eyes. *A lifetime.* Had she heard right? "I can get on board with that," she uttered through the heart in her throat.

His brows shot heavenward, and he pulled her into a fierce hug, stroking her hair. "Are you sure?"

Before she could respond, Gina's phone chanted, "A biotch is calling. A biotch is calling,"

Austin sputtered into laughter.

"Oh, my God. I'm going to kill my sister." She tapped the screen. "What?"

"I guess you're not having as good a time as we are," Cyndi teased. "We've covered the whole first floor, including the kitchen–don't ask. Anyway, Duke isn't here yet. After you pull on your panties, check on him, will you?"

Gina rolled her eyes. "I need to find my panties before I can put them on."

"Oh." Cyndi squeaked.

"We'll see you down there soon." Gina hung up with a frown.

Austin glanced at his watch, tapping the face. "It's time."

"Fine." They'd been talking about a future together, but whatever. Lack of sleep or sex–probably both–had her emotions all over the place. She reached for the doorknob, but Austin caught her hand.

"Our conversation isn't over." He tipped her chin, so she met his gaze. "Only paused." He wore a sexy grin.

"Promise?"

"I do."

With a stiff nod, she blinked through the unshed tears and stymied her excitement to focus on the task at hand: meeting Duke and her friends.

"Cyndi said Duke isn't downstairs yet."

Austin opened the door. "We can check his room before we go to the lobby."

Gina crossed to the author's room and rapped her knuckles on the door. The door pushed open a crack. She glanced toward Austin. "We closed this when we left. Do you think he forgot to shut it if he went downstairs?"

Frowning, Austin rubbed his chin. "I don't know. Something feels off." He reached out and pushed the door. The room was dark as he stepped inside.

"Be careful," Gina softly uttered.

Austin flipped the closest light switch. "Oh no," he groaned. "Duke!" Austin surged forward.

Gina zeroed in on a pair of legs poking out from between the beds. The room spun. She leaned against the wall, squeezing her eyes shut. Her chest heaved.

"Is he dead?" The words tumbled from her mouth, but she didn't recognize the voice.

"No."

"Thank God." She pulled in a ragged breath, then another, before opening her eyes.

Austin kneeled, a grim expression pinched his features. The valley between the beds swallowed his torso as he bent over Duke.

"He's hurt. There's a bloody goose egg on his head, and he's out cold." Austin met Gina's gaze. "I need to call the cops."

"Poor Duke," Gina murmured, peeking over the edge of the bed. She gasped and recoiled, turning quickly.

"Are you alright?" Austin asked, coming to her side. He had his phone in his hand.

"Better than he is. Go ahead and call. We need to get him some help." Gina gulped back the sour taste in her throat as Austin punched in the number for the police.

She texted her sister.

We found Duke unconscious in his room. He has a large bump on his head. We'll stay until help arrives.

The little bubbles appeared, signaling Cyndi's reply. *Was he assaulted, or did he fall?*

Gina blinked at the screen. Had he fallen? Was it possible Duke had an accident? She turned, inspecting the room in a new light. The one bed was disheveled, and the table was untidy but remained just as before. His shoes had been kicked out of the direct pathway.

But the door had been ajar.

An uneasiness settled in her gut. She walked to the window and turned, taking in the entire room. Duke's banner and a plethora of totes sat in a tower next to the armoire with the safe.

"Oh!" she squeaked, pointing to the empty safe.

Still on the phone, Austin glanced where she pointed.

"The laptop. It's gone."

Chapter 18

Austin

"What do you mean, gone?" I asked, placing a pillow under Duke's head. I stood and inspected the empty safe. "Who do you think took it?"

"Whoever it was hit poor Duke over the head, knocked him out, and stole the computer before anyone saw them." Gina was firm on her accusation.

"But who?" I asked, while grabbing a washcloth from the bathroom and returning to Duke's side. I gently pressed it against the bloody goose egg on the back of his head. Then turned my attention to Gina.

With her pinched expression, I knew what she was thinking.

"Anybody could have known Duke had the laptop," she speculated.

Noise from the hallway drew our attention. The door to Duke's room opened and a slew of people rushed inside. We were urged aside by the EMTs. The paramedics took no time to set his neck in a brace and had him on a gurney.

They carried him out of the room, leaving us with Officer Cox.

"Now, tell me what happened." Cox pulled out her notebook. She looked at Gina and me with exasperation.

"We wanted to talk to Duke, and when we approached his door, it was already open. We found him unconscious with a bump on his head," I explained.

"That's it?" Cox looked up from her notepad, her eyes searching my face.

"That's it," Gina confirmed.

"Was there anyone in the hallway?"

"No one except for us."

Cox nodded, shoved the notebook into her breast pocket, and let out an irritated breath. "If you remember anything else, you got my card."

"Actually, I gave the card to Molly. She was supposed to call you with important details about Deidra Raines."

"Well, she hasn't contacted me yet. What does she need to tell me?"

"There are rumors about Rod Stiff plagiarizing from other authors, and Molly said Deidra Raines hated the man for just that. She also assumed Harrison and Rod were sleeping and working together."

Cox harrumphed, shaking her head. "That's all speculation. Does she have proof?"

"I don't know," I admitted, looking at Gina, who shrugged.

"Okay. This is what I'll do. I'm going to go track down Ms. Raines' PA and talk to her. But please, if you hear anyone who has concrete backing for Molly's accusations, call me." She pats her pockets. "Crap. I ran out of cards–well, I'll be around here for a while longer."

"Oh, wait," Gina called out as Officer Cox paused mid-step.

I looked at Gina, who focused on the cop. "We think whoever hurt Mr. Wain stole something out of his safe."

"And what do you think the attacker took?"

Gina looked at me, and I nodded for her to go on. "Duke is Harrison Busch's father, and he took Rod Stiff's laptop yesterday. We think the attacker knew Duke had it. This attacker might be the same person that killed Mr. Stiff and possibly Chad."

The wide-eyed look on Cox's face was almost comical. But I kept my opinion to myself.

"Well, I wish I knew that bit of information earlier." She eyeballed us both. "How long have you known or kept this detail from me?"

I swallowed hard. "Duke told us earlier today," I said evenly, keeping my eyes on the cop. I didn't want her to think we were intentionally hiding any evidence, or be an accessory for holding pertinent information.

"Austin is telling the truth. Duke told us he took the laptop because he was afraid Harrison would be blamed for Stiff's murder," Gina explained with vehemence. "Duke also thinks what's on the laptop could show Harrison's innocence to Rodney Stiff's murder."

Cox pulled out her phone and started texting away. "Is that everything?"

"Yes," Gina and I said at the same time.

"Alright then. Now that it's done, I'm heading to look for Molly." With that, the officer left the room.

Taking Gina's hand, I pulled her out into the hallway and closed the door. I was ready to escort my girl to my room, but she lightly yanked on my arm.

"It's already time to get ready for the after-party. I need

166 Rochelle Bradley & CJ Warrant

to meet up with the Babes," she said with a sad smile. A ping from a text interrupted us. She glanced at her screen. "It's the group chat. The girls are coming up to get dressed. I have to go."

I pulled her in for a hug, knowing how she was feeling. "Don't be sad. We'll have plenty of time to be together." I rubbed at her back.

"I know, but it's more than that. I'm worried about Duke. All this... this event was supposed to be fun. I came here for the books and to hang with my sister and friends. I wasn't ready to be embroiled in a murder–two murders."

I squeezed her tighter to me. "Look on the bright side. If you hadn't come, we wouldn't have reconnected. And my life would be miserable." I looked into her beautiful watery gaze. "I'm glad you're back in my life, Gina. And if I have to go through another ten more ordeals like this, I would. Because you are worth it."

"Oh, Philly." She wrapped her arms around my neck and pulled me down for a hot, demanding kiss that didn't last as long as I wanted. "Will I see you later?"

"I'll meet you at the party. I'm going to check on Redd. The last thing we need is for him to go half-cocked and do something totally stupid."

Gina got in the elevator with a few familiar authors. Once the door slid closed, I started toward Redd's room when I got a text from the man himself.

Redd: *I go swimin.*

Oh, hell no. I booked it to the pool on the second floor. I didn't bother with the elevator and took the stairs two steps at a time. The moment I stormed inside the humid area, I frantically inspected the pool. Much to my relief, I didn't see Redd floating ass-up in the water.

From the adjacent bathroom, someone groaned. I

rushed inside and found Redd crammed in a stall, ass on the floor, and the empty bottle of Jack between his legs.

Redd tipped his head back and squinted up at me. "Come in," he slurred. "Join the part-tay."

"Come on, big guy. Let me help you to your room." I reached out a hand, but he batted it away.

"No. I'm good."

"You can't stay here, Redd. Take my hand," I insisted.

Redd narrowed his gaze on my hand before letting out a foul-smelling fart. With a chuckle, he lifted a cell phone with a cracked screen to his face. "Did that sound wet to you, Chad?" he sobbed.

"Jesus H. Christ." I quickly dropped my hand and jumped away from the stall. "I'm going to wait for you out there."

Redd called out my name as I was about to leave the bathroom.

With reluctance, I turned around and slowly stepped back into the bathroom. As Redd appeared in my line of sight, he was getting up with the help of the toilet.

He swung around on his heels and teetered backward out of the stall, the empty bottle of Jack in his right hand. I supported him to the elevator and up to his room.

As I helped him take off his clothes, I said, "I'm assuming you're not going to the after-party?"

He wiped his mouth with the back of his hand and then burped. "No fucking way. Not without Chad. It won't feel right to go without him. Would you go without your girl?"

"Redd—"

"No man. Can't you see how devastating this is for me?" His eyes were filled with tears as he grabbed the cell phone off the table and waved it at me. "I will never forget this man."

"How about you get into bed and try to get a good night's sleep? And we'll talk tomorrow," I suggested, hoping Redd would comply.

He dropped his arm, slumped to the bed, and got under the covers without complaint.

I tucked him in and was about to leave when Redd called my name. "Do you know how lucky I am to find this phone in the bathroom? I will forever keep this near my heart, knowing Chad is right here with me." He then closed his eyes and started snoring.

Not his phone?

Redd's home screen had a picture of his mother and him. I took a step toward the bed to get a better look at the phone in his hand. Redd had it clutched to his chest, and I couldn't see it. Then, with a gentle nudge, the big man turned, his arm flopped out of the blanket, exposing the phone.

This could be evidence.

Using the hotel's cup's plastic wrapper, I cautiously coax the phone out of his grip. I tapped on the cracked screen, wanting to see what Redd was talking about. Sure enough, the second the lock screen blinked on, Chad appeared in a bed, wearing nothing but a sultry smile.

Now to answer the question: *who does this phone belong to?*

Chapter 19

Gina

Brandy rushed into the bathroom, blocking Gina's view of the mirror. She added detail to her lion nose.

"Missed a spot," Gina teased, edging in beside her, eyeliner in hand.

"Did not." Brandy frowned, leaning over the counter and going cross-eyed as she examined her nose.

"Who wants curls?" Cyndi called from the other room.

"Ooh, me!" Brandy shuffled out of the bathroom and disappeared around the corner, leaving Gina alone to apply her makeup.

Cyndi had already fixed Gina's Dorothy Gale braided ponytails with bright red bows. Gina finished her makeup and swirled her checkered blue and white gingham dress. Satisfied she could pass as an acceptable Dorothy, Gina went to help her friends with their costumes.

"What can I do to help?" Gina asked, entering Cyndi and Sam's room. Her sister held a portion of Brandy's hair out, then used a curling iron.

"You can help me," Sam called from her bathroom.

"My zipper is stuck." She walked out in a fuchsia layered skirt, a little longer than a tutu. Glittery translucent wings were affixed to the back of the gumball pink bodysuit. She held a wand with a glowing star tip.

"Can't you wish it unstuck?" Brandy laughed.

"Ha ha." Hands on her hips, she tapped her high-heeled pink boots.

"What are you? Some sort of street-walking fairy?" Gina asked.

Sam rolled her eyes. "I'm Glinda the Good Witch, you dirty-minded-flying-monkey."

"If you only had a brain," Cyndi sang, wiggling jazz fingers on her free hand.

"Hey, let's focus on my mane," Brandy said to Cyndi.

"Somebody's found their courage." Sam pointed her wand at Brandy.

"Yes, your royal-pain-in-the-butt." Cyndi continued to work on curling Brandy's hair. She arranged the Goldilocks' curls, clipped a red bow on the side, and sprayed hairspray.

"Looks like we are waiting for you, scarecrow." Gina handed Cyndi a flannel shirt with yellow yarn hanging out of the arms and chest pocket.

Cyndi grabbed the shirt and slid it on over her tank top. She shimmied out of her fleece pajama shorts and then pulled on a pair of oversized brown pants with a few faux burlap patches.

"Hey, Sam. Let's open the blush wine I won from the LaShanda Rose's giveaway," Brandy suggested. "And you can help me clip my tail onto my fanny pack. I want to make sure it's centered."

"You don't have to ask me twice. It's always wine o'clock somewhere." Sam followed Brandy into the other room. Gina heard cellophane crinkle, and her friends chattered excitedly about the prize.

Cyndi tugged her hair into a bun and secured it with bobby pins. She lowered her voice so only Gina could hear, "So, spill the beans about Austin. Did you...? Is he as fine as he looks? Is he the hardcover edition?"

Gina's face flared hot, and she met her sister's gaze in the mirror. She swallowed her disappointment and expectations. "We haven't exactly..." She shrugged and her gaze dropped to the floor.

"What?" Cyndi gasped, spinning around. "Does he think you're not good enough for him?"

Gina's gaze snapped to her twin. She shook her head. "Of course not. Philly isn't like that. We haven't had the opportunity... yet." She sighed. "I'm sure it will be just as hot as he is."

"Good. I'd have to kick his ass if he was playing you." Cyndi nodded and turned her attention back to arranging her hair. "But you've had a few opportunities–"

"We were interrupted time and again. Screaming, mayhem, unsolicited visitors..." Gina shook her head. She took a seat on the edge of the bed, remembering Austin's fingers stroking her sensitive nub. A shiver of heat pooled in her core as she crossed her legs, longing for uninterrupted alone time with the man she was falling for.

"Maybe you will have some fun after the party." Cyndi wiggled her brows. "Goodness knows one of us should get some." She lowered a pointed fabric hat over her head.

A smile lodged itself on Gina's face, and she gladly accepted the plastic cup of blush wine Sam handed her. "You two look great together. I can't wait to see what costume Austin will wear."

"Me too," Gina sighed and took a sip of the wine.

"Well, let's finish getting ready. There's partying to be had," Brandy cheered.

When they finally left their rooms, they waited excitedly for the elevator to arrive. The doors opened, and they saw Duke Wain. Gina leaped forward, happy to see the conscious author.

The Babes followed her. "Oh crap, we are going up," Cyndi observed.

"Duke, how are you feeling?" Brandy asked, touching his arm.

"Could be better. I have some painkillers I can take for later. But you gals look spectacular."

"Do you need help?" Gina asked, feeling sorry for the older man.

"No..." His words faltered as he took a wobbly step backward. "Maybe I do."

"You need to lie down for a while," Sam suggested.

"Sam is right, Mr. Wain. You are slightly pale," Cyndi added with a touch to his arm.

"Maybe you're right. An hour nap should help this Wizard feel a bit better," Duke confessed.

"If you want, we can sit with you?" Gina offered.

"No. You four go and have fun. I'll be down in an hour. Save me a seat?" Duke looked at Gina.

"You know it," Brandy boomed, which made Duke wince. "Sorry."

The Babes waved goodbye to Duke and pushed the L. The lobby was filled with all sorts of Wizard of Oz characters. From several Dorothys to the flying monkeys. Even the Wicked Witch of the East's henchmen guards.

With this much frivolity, one would never guess two murders had taken place in the hotel. And maybe that was a good thing. Who would want a dour, dreary party?

Gina practically skipped into the ballroom with her sister and friends in tow. A photo booth complete with props caught their attention, and they moseyed over to the line. Heavenly smells from the baked potato bar, nacho buffet, and other food swirled in the air.

"Look at the bar." Sam pointed to the whiskey-lined shelves and two bartenders meeting the needs of thirsty readers and authors.

Green lights glowed on either side of the parquet dance floor. "Look at the floor. It's the yellow brick road." Brandy motioned to where gold tape lined a walkway to the center of the room.

As they edged closer to the front of the line, the Boba Book Babes enjoyed spotting characters from the Wizard of Oz.

"Keeley Wetstone's lion costume is epic. A makeup artist from Cats must have painted her face. And that body-suit..." Brandy glanced down at her tawny knee-length dress and tan booties with a frown.

"Don't worry about it. You look cute." Sam gave Brandy a side-hug, then gently yanked her tail.

"That's appropriate." Cyndi snickered as she nodded her head in Tammy's direction.

"No kidding," Gina agreed.

Near the DJ booth, Tammy stood wearing green face paint, a black robe, and a pointy hat. Her long, dagger-like fingernails glinted in the green light. "I'm going to get you, my pretty." She pointed to the volunteer Ruby, who wore a gingham dress and a dark wig. She carried a picnic basket with a stuffed corgi.

"Oh no, Toto, it's the Wicked Witch of the West." Ruby chortled.

Sam tugged on Gina's sleeve. "There's another witch."

"It's the *bitch* witch." Brandy snorted, and the Boba Babes giggled.

"How did Jackie talk all the Boozy Bitch bloggers into being flying monkeys?" Cyndi shook her head.

"The jury is out on that one," Gina quipped.

"They are her minions," Sam offered with a one-shoulder shrug.

The group in front of them posed for pictures with wanted signs and other props. They switched positions between flashes.

Gina leaned close to her sister and softly said, "Some of these costumes hide the faces. Doesn't it make you nervous with a murderer or two on the loose?"

Cyndi took Gina's hands and gave her a reassuring squeeze. "It does, but look around. There are security goons at the doors, plus a few uniformed officers patrolling the emerald city."

Gina sighed and nodded, then hugged Cyndi. "Thanks. I'll feel better when Austin gets here."

"Is he still babysitting Redd?" Cyndi asked, as they scrambled to find props for the photo booth.

"No. Austin tucked Redd into bed, then went to get ready for the party. He should be here soon." Gina grabbed a pair of oversized sunglasses.

Brandy slapped a pair of plastic handcuffs on her wrists while Sam held the wanted sign up like a mugshot. Cyndi rummaged through the cardboard cutouts and found a ball gag. She raised it to Brandy's mouth, and the Babes busted out laughing.

"Perfect," Cyndi grinned as the camera flashed.

Brandy, a ball gag, and handcuffs. That would be an interesting Clue game.

They posed and then waited for the printer to spit out

their pictures. Giggling, they found an empty round table. It was about forty-five minutes later when Gina saw Duke strolling into the party. He gave her a wave and then grabbed himself a drink.

"Let's eat before the Boozy bitches gobble everything." Brandy scanned the potato bar where a hotel employee refilled the shredded cheese container.

"I'm heading to the most important bar. Anybody want something to drink?" Sam studied a bright sign with neon green letters. "Oh, there's a special Pandemonium in Peoria event drink too."

"I'll take one," Gina said, handing a twenty to Sam. Once Brandy and Sam left, Gina turned to her sister. "I'm probably not going to return to the hotel room with you tonight."

Cyndi's brows shot upward. "Oh? It's about time."

Gina's body heated. "If I'm lucky. And I plan to get lucky..." She glanced around the room, then turned back to her twin. "I have a foolproof plan to finish what we started all those years ago."

"What plan?"

Gina grinned as she slid her finger under the collar of her dress and pulled out her bra strap. The blood-red lace shimmered in the ambient light.

"Pretty and sexy." Cyndi cooed.

"And I have a matching thong," Gina smirked. She'd get Austin naked for some private time.

"I'll hang the 'do not disturb' sign or, better yet, spray paint if this door's a-rockin' don't come a-knockin'."

Sam returned with the drinks. "This is heavenly, y'all." She sipped the green concoction and hummed.

"Let's get some food. Divide and conquer?" Cyndi asked Gina pointedly. "I'll hit the potato bar."

Gina nodded. "Sure. I'll get a heap of nachos—"

"With all the fixin's," Sam interrupted.

"And I'll get you each a potato. Is butter, sour cream, cheese, and bacon okay?"

Sam grinned. "Everything's better with butter."

"And bacon," Gina added, then fist-bumped Sam.

Cyndi wove through the tables in the opposite direction of Gina while Sam trailed her, offering to hold the fixin's plate.

As Gina piled the nacho chips onto a white plate, she caught Sam's puzzled expression. She stared openly at the closest table. Gina scanned the women and found nothing threatening. "What's wrong?" she finally asked.

"Some of these costumes are weird. Like that bronze robot and girl with the white face." Sam shook her head and loaded her plate with salsa, guacamole, and shredded cheese.

"It's Tik-Tok," Gina offered. "She did an awesome job on her costume."

Sam scrunched her face in thought. "TikTok, the social media platform?"

Gina stopped moving and lowered her plate to the buffet. "Don't you know who Tik-Tok is?" When Sam blinked, Gina continued, "He is a character in L. Frank Baum's book series."

"Who?"

Others in the line stopped, some openly gaping at Sam. Gina pinched the bridge of her nose. "Frank is the author of the Wizard of Oz series of books."

"It's a book?" Sam rubbed her chin. "Well, that explains why it's the theme. Wait, there's more than one?"

"There are more than a dozen," a woman dressed as a good witch chimed in.

"Dorothy's slippers are supposed to be silver," another added.

Sam glanced at Gina's strappy red high heels, then met her gaze with an arched brow. "I know, but I wanted my shoes to match my bows," Gina said with a shrug. *And my underwear.*

The Boba Babes sampled the variety of food while comparing costumes and trying to figure out who was behind the makeup and masks.

Gina checked her phone again. Austin's lack of communication gnawed at her nerves. Brandy nudged her, and she started. "What?"

"Your book boyfriend is here." Brandy pointed near the photo booth.

As Gina panned the crowd, she spotted Austin standing, hands on hips. Even his brooding expression didn't deter from his chiseled features. His intense gaze searched the tables.

Gina stood, catching his attention. When he saw her, his eyes softened, and his jaw relaxed. He stalked through the crowd like a lion after its prey. She rubbed her stomach, trying to still the butterflies dancing around inside. The closer he came, the wider his smile grew.

"Gina," he said, pulling her into his arms.

For a moment, she closed her eyes and lost herself in his strong embrace. She buried her face in his T-shirt, smelling soap and clean linen with a hint of whisky. She sighed, holding him tight.

"Get a room," Cyndi mumbled, then chomped on a nacho.

Gina opened her eyes and raised a one-finger salute to her older twin.

"I've missed you," she whispered for his ears only.

"I've missed you, too." Austin kissed her head and squeezed her before letting go. His voice lowered, turning serious. "I've got to show you something."

"Here you go, Austin," Brandy said, scooting over one seat so he could sit next to Gina.

They slipped into the chairs. Sam pushed the almost empty nacho plate toward Austin. "Thanks." He used a large chip to scoop some bean dip, took a bite, and grimaced.

"Tastes like butt, right?" Sam laughed.

"I think it's more like dirty socks," Brandy added with a shrug.

Austin gulped and took a sip of the water Gina handed him. He emptied the glass.

"What do you need to show me?" she asked.

Austin fished something out of his back pocket and set it on the table. A plastic bag covered a small dark object. He flipped it over.

"Is that a phone?" Gina asked, leaning in and inspecting it.

"Yes. Redd found it in the men's bathroom near the pool. It's not his, but he wouldn't let it go until he fell asleep. Don't touch it."

The group of women stared at the small device. "Why not?" Cyndi asked, cocking a brow.

"I used the plastic surrounding a glass to pick it up. It could be Harrison's," Austin suggested.

Gina pinched the plastic and pulled it loose. The spider-webbed screen appeared to have been shattered by a blunt object. She used the plastic to push the large button lighting the home screen. Chad lounging in bed, a white sheet covering his groin, stared at her. She gasped, recalling his vacant eyes and pale face.

"Hello, gorgeous," Brandy said, looking at the picture.

"That looks familiar." Cyndi tapped her chin.

Austin rubbed Gina's back, snapping her out of her bleak thoughts. She pushed through her last memory of Chad and sifted through images like a slideshow in her mind. Sexy men on book covers.

"Ah-ha!" Gina jabbed a finger in the air. "I know where this picture of Chad is from."

"You do?" Sam asked. "Well, don't just sit there all pretty. Spill the beans."

With a grin, Gina saluted. She placed her palms on the table and waited until her friends and sister leaned close. "It's from Rodney Stiff's newest book. The one that's on pre-order." She gasped again and flipped it over, careful not to touch the phone. She recognized the purple case. "Oh. My. God."

Cyndi, Sam, and Brandy stared at her wide-eyed.

"What is it?" Cyndi asked, covering her sister's hand and squeezing.

Gina's heart hammered in her chest, and she covered it, trying to keep it in place. She found the air stifling and couldn't breathe.

"Breathe, Gina." Austin rubbed her back. "Keep your eyes on me, and take a breath."

His warmth fortified her. She drew a deep, cleansing breath and glanced around the room. The short person in the Tik-Tok costume passed their table. They didn't wear any shoes and had several small blue tattoos on one ankle. Her vibe tingled. Gina blinked and took another deep, cleansing breath.

"I've seen this phone before. It belonged to Rodney Stiff." She glanced around the table at the Boba Babes' stunned faces.

"Holy shit," Austin murmured. "We need to get this to Officer Cox." He jumped to his feet.

"Excuse me." A man's booming voice came from the DJ's booth. The reverb screeched. "Sorry about that. Welcome to the Pandemonium in Peoria after-party. Here is your hostess with the mostess: Tammy Shaver."

The crowd clapped and whistled.

Tammy smiled and curtseyed. "Thank you. We have a few announcements before we start the dance music. First, I'd like to thank our volunteers. If you volunteered in any way, please stand."

She began clapping as people rose. Some waved, others bowed.

The room broke out in deafening cheers.

Austin dropped into his chair again. "I'll wait until after the hubbub."

Tammy continued, "Izzy and her team... You've done a fabulous job on the raffle baskets. Didn't they?" Her pointy hat shifted as she tilted her head.

The applause and hoots hurt Gina's ears. Especially Cyndi's exuberant whistle.

"Speaking of the raffle..." Tammy paused dramatically as Izzy trotted to her side in a colorful horse costume, "we will start drawing the winners soon."

"That's right, Tammy. Who's ready to win? We'll begin the drawing at eight." Izzy swirled.

"That will give all you pretties plenty of time to eat, drink, and dance," Tammy added like the Wicked Witch of the West, rubbing her hands together.

"And..." Izzy bounced forward, coming close to the Boba Babes' table, "it will give us a chance to raise more money for the charity. That's right. We are having a last minute ticket sale."

"No!" Cyndi vaulted out of her seat. Everyone gawked at her. Her gaze hopped from table to table, then to Izzy. Gina's sister's demeanor shifted from crazed to nonchalance. "I mean, oh, no, I left my wallet in my room."

Undeterred, Izzy beamed. "That's alright. You have time to go get your money."

Cyndi dropped into her seat once more, a deep frown carved in her face.

Brandy wore a smirk. "Nice recovery."

"Really, Cyndi." Gina tsked. "Haven't you spent enough on the Jamison Blaine package?"

"If Austin was in a basket, what would you pay?" Cyndi asked, her shoulders slumped as she crossed her arms.

Gina placed a possessive hand on Austin's leg. She'd give everything, but they'd known each other before. Jamison was a stranger to Cyndi. *Apples to oranges.*

Tammy droned on about the event, trying to avoid the negative. Brandy listened intently. Sam motioned toward the bar and went for a second drink.

"How long is the windbag going to talk?" Austin groused.

Cyndi nudged Gina in the side. "Look at Sam."

They all focused on their friend. She stood beside the bar and waved. Once she'd noticed she had their attention, Sam tipped her head and shook it as if to get water out of her ear.

Brandy sat up straight. "Look who's at the bar now."

"Deidra Raines," Austin stated.

"They let her out. She must not be the killer." Cyndi studied the small woman.

Deidra turned with a fruity concoction in each hand. Deep circles etched her eyes, amplified by the smeared mascara. As if her battery was on reserve power, she ambled toward the table in the darkest corner.

"Now, let's start the party. Maestro," Tammy motioned toward the DJ, who amped up the music. Bass pumped, and Izzy started to prance to the rhythm.

"Finally," Austin murmured.

A woman yelled. "Look!"

"Woohoo." A munchkin clapped her hands.

"Yeah, baby," another hollered. Several women jumped to their feet and clapped to the beat.

The group focused on the door where a man in nothing but a rainbow jock had entered, screaming. He ran toward the dance floor in the center of the ballroom. Then he stopped, bent over, hands on his knees, wheezing.

"They hired a stripper? This is new." Brandy craned her neck.

"There's nothing to strip except that rainbow sparkly marble sack between his legs," Cyndi snickered at her observation.

Gina strained to see the thin man's face. Dried blood lined his cheek, arms, and legs. The DJ cut the song. "Oh my God, that's Harrison Busch."

Chapter 20

Gina

"Harrison Busch," a winged monkey gasped from the table behind the Book Babes.

"Harrison Busch," a man's voice echoed from the shadows.

Hearing his name, he spun. Harrison's lips were swollen and one eye black. Several small puncture marks on his thighs leaked blood.

"Where is that frumpy bitch?" Spittle flew out of his mouth. His wild gaze scrutinized the crowd.

Austin rose, standing protectively between Gina and the crazed man. "Who are–"

"That bitch, Molly Caudill." He growled. "That brown-nosing she-devil kidnapped me. She locked me up. Look what she did to me. I'm going to kill her–"

"Harrison, are you alright?" Austin asked, cautiously taking a step forward.

He rolled his eyes. "No, you dipshit. I've been slapped around like daddy's little bitch. She beat me with a hardback journal and then stabbed me with a swag pen. Look at me, asshole, I'm bleeding." He swept his arm over his body.

"Harrison Busch," Redd shrieked as he barreled toward the man. "I'm going to kill you."

Austin moved to intercept but missed.

"Ah–help!" Harrison squealed like a child as he tried to dodge the angry man. Redd collided with him. They crashed to the floor and slid to a stop before the DJ.

Harrison's mouth opened and closed like a fish. Redd pushed up and raised his fist. "You killed the man I loved," he roared.

"Help! Somebody call my lawyer. Get this moose off me." Harrison squirmed, pinned under Redd's enormous frame.

Austin caught Redd's fist. "Come on, big guy. Let him up. This isn't you."

Redd snarled. "No way. This bastard killed Chad."

"Gross, you smell like a haunted refinery." Then Harrison froze. "What does he mean? I didn't... Chad's dead?" Harrison's face turned sheet white when Redd's words hit him. "I would never–"

Austin pulled Redd off the small man, but he tried to go after Harrison again. "Stop, Redd, before the cops arrest you for assault," he warned his friend.

"Where is he–where's my Chad?" Harrison cried out. He kicked and squirmed as Duke, Izzy, and a few others pulled him free while Austin held Redd back. He climbed to his feet.

"You lying bastard," Redd spat.

Harrison shook his head as wetness filled his eyes. "No," escaped in a hoarse whisper. The tears overflowed, leaving clean trails on his face. "He... I... He can't be dead."

He jammed his fingers into his hair, then covered his face with his palms. "I loved him."

Gina crept to Austin's side. "Molly did this to you?" she uttered in disbelief.

"Yes." He wiped his face, then balled his fists. "She must have killed Chad, too."

Gina met Austin's gaze before asking Harrison, "How do you know?"

"Honey, Chad told me he saw her sneaking away from the panel stage with a basket full of hard candy dicks. He assumed she'd killed Rodney. Molly said Chad tried to bribe her, so he wouldn't go to the cops." Harrison waved his hand. "Besides, nobody is sad Rod is dead. Nobody in the industry except his publisher, that is. Rod was a swindler and a plagiarist. Ask any author. But Chad..." His glassy eyes turned hard.

Molly had visited Austin's room, too. Would she have killed Gina's man? She shivered and took hold of his hand.

Duke offered Harrison his green wizard vest. He slipped it on, looking like a flamboyant leprechaun.

Harrison limped to the edge of the dance floor. He cupped his wild eyes, scouring the crowd. "Where the hell is that evil shrew?"

The crowd murmured. Heads swiveled as animated conversations broke out. Cox and another uniformed officer stormed onto the dance floor. "Harrison Busch. Where the hell have you been? We have questions regarding the murders of Rodney Stiff and Chad Cummings," Cox demanded.

"Get in line," Harrison grunted, refusing to give up on the search. He stopped beside Brandy, who tugged on her mane.

Cox huffed and put a hand on her belt. She pointed to

a couple of women with their phones recording the ordeal. "I'll need those videos."

"Your leg is still bleeding. You should probably go to the hospital and let the cops handle Molly," Cyndi suggested to Harrison.

His glare landed on Cyndi, and his lip curled in a snarl. "Not until..." His gaze dropped to the table. "That's Rodney's phone." He reached for it, but Cyndi covered it with her napkin.

"Careful. Fingerprints," she warned.

"Rodney Stiff's phone was found near the pool," Austin told Cox as she hustled to the table.

"John," she called into her shoulder radio. "We need an evidence kit." She turned to Gina. "Where exactly?"

"Redd found it," Austin said.

They all glanced at Redd, who reclined on the parquet floor, staring at the ceiling, tears streaming from his eyes.

"He's hammered," Austin added the obvious.

Detective Burns muscled his way past the gawkers. "Harrison Busch–"

"Yeah, yeah, you want to talk to me." He waved his hand. "I'm flattered. Really, I am, but listen up, buttercup: I need to find that murdering nitwit before she bails."

Burns' brow furrowed. "Which nitwit would that be?"

Cox rolled her eyes. She briefly summed up Harrison and Redd's exchange. When others joined them, Redd was escorted out of the ballroom and the phone photographed and then zipped inside a bag.

Harrison sagged against a chair back. He zeroed in on the corner cast in shadow.

Gina offered the wounded man a glass of water. He gave her a fleeting grin before returning to his task.

"Molly, that little slip of a thing tied you up?" the detective asked.

"Yep. After Chad left my room, she knocked on my door and said she had information to expose Rodney for the scum he really was." Harrison rubbed his forehead. "I was intrigued. She wore owl pajamas. And I was like, 'oh no, honey, Miss Kitty is barking up the wrong tree.' Then she told me she had Rod's laptop—which is missing, by the way—"

Gina, Austin, and the Boba Babes glanced at Duke, whose wince remained unnoticed by his son.

"Her room smelled of feet and cheese." Harrison shivered, then gagged. "She whacked me on the head and threatened me with a knife. After she tied me up, I noticed the blood. I thought it was part of the pajama design. I yelled for help, and she stuck a nasty sock in my mouth and duct taped it there." He dry-heaved again. "God, she was angry. Angry at Rod for stealing her ideas and printing them. Angry at me for doing nothing to stop him. Angry at Deidra for paying her so poorly and–," Harrison huffed out a sneer. "Angry at those Boozy Bitch Bitches for the horrid review they wrote about Rodney's book, which was actually Molly's idea."

Jackie jumped to her feet. "That twat sabotaged our basket."

Gina held Austin's hand and squeezed.

How did he land on Molly's shit list?

Harrison pointed to Austin like he'd read her mind. "Since your girl was on the police's radar as a suspect, Molly planned to woo you and... Ssst." He made a motion with a finger across his throat. "You were next, Austin."

Gina met Cyndi's wide-eyed gaze. No wonder Molly visited Austin's room. It had nothing to do with Deidra but implicating Gina as the murderer by killing Austin. She threw her arms around his waist and never wanted to let him go.

"How do you know all of these things?" Detective Burns asked Harrison.

"God save me. The woman loved to monologue. While she stuck me with a pen, slapped me with a book, and tried to pry those tacky boots off her stanky, tattooed feet, she went on and on about how she'd made Rodney pay."

Gina's eyes shifted to the police officers who roamed the perimeter of the large room. All the while, the costumed readers and authors hung on to every word of Harrison's story.

Wherever Molly hid, she was either lucky enough to have crept away early, or she remained hidden within the partygoers.

Gina sucked in a breath, remembering the women's conversation in the bathroom before Barb's scream.

"Everything will be alright. You'll see." Then Gina remembered the pale blue raindrop tattoo on the right ankle next to her stall. *"I'm going to kill that SOB and make him pay for what he's done."*

Gina had seen the same tattoo during dinner around the nacho bar. It had to have been Molly who gorged herself on the chips and a mound of cheese.

Scanning the room again, Gina saw Molly in the corner by the nacho buffet—a small-statured person in a pristine Tik-Tok costume. If she weren't a murdering nutcase, Gina would commend Molly for her costume perfection.

"I know where Molly is," Gina whispered to Austin.

Hearing like a curious cat, Cox stuck her head between the couple. "Where?" the cop whispered.

"Have you ever read the Oz books?" Gina asked.

Cox frowned. "I've seen the movie."

All the readers within earshot sighed and shook their heads. Gina released Austin and pulled out her phone. After tapping her screen, she found the book depicting the steampunk-like bronzed robot. "She's dressed like this."

Cox scanned the area and pointed to the table. Officers moved to intercept the group, especially the closest one to the food.

"That's not her," Gina berated. She turned so her back was toward Molly. "The round table near the other end of the nacho bar. She's on the right side."

Cox's narrowed gaze homed in on the table. "Which one? They're all bronzed robots."

A moment later, Gina's hair fluttered as a steak knife whizzed past. Austin spun Gina out of the way. He held her for a nanosecond before dropping to a crouch. Harrison squealed and ducked. The sharp cutlery landed on the wood floor with a metallic scrape.

Detective Burns, Cox and the surrounding officers sprang into action, rushing for Molly. She pushed over the nacho buffet, sending a flood of liquid cheese onto the floor. Her costume inhibited her from moving spryly, and the officers apprehended her near the photo booth.

The reporter, Tanya Fitzpatrick, while interviewing guests, got caught up in the melee. In Molly's pursuit, Tanya was pushed, slipping on her heels and falling into the mess. Aghast, she sat up covered head to toe in cheese.

Molly swung her arms and kicked, while screaming, "I'm innocent, damn it! It was all an accident. Let me go, you assholes. They deserved it."

"You tried to kill my sister, you stupid author wanna-be," Cyndi yelled.

"She can get her mugshot here," Sam said, pointing to the photo booth.

"That's not funny," Brandy chided, then busted out laughing. "Yes, it is."

"It wouldn't be funny if that knife cut Gina," Austin growled.

The two Babes snapped their mouths shut.

Breathing heavily, Gina rested her head against Austin's shoulder. She tried to ignore Molly's shrieks and pleas. Austin's strong heartbeat pounded under her hand. All she wanted was for the ordeal to end and alone time with her man.

Tammy tapped on the mic. "Excuse me. Those who have videos of everything that transpired, please see the police officer at this table." The officer waved, and witches, monkeys, Dorothy, and her friends lined up to pass on their evidence.

"One more thing. Tickets are now on sale..."

"God bless America," Cyndi groaned, throwing her hands into the air in frustration.

Austin tried to suppress his laughter, but the vibrations tickled Gina. Soon she giggled along with him.

Chapter 21

Austin

Watching Molly being hauled away was slightly satisfying since she killed not only Rodney Stiff but also Chad. No matter her reasons for killing those two men, it wasn't right. She could have easily gone to the police. But she chose the path of murder. And now she was going to spend her life behind bars.

I hated to admit it, but the reporter covered in gooey cheese had made me laugh. However, Tanya's face reflected humiliation mixed with anger, which I didn't blame her. She let out a shrill scream before storming out of the hotel.

I glanced at Gina, whose eyes were on her frazzled sister. The second Tammy called out that they were still selling tickets, I swore Cyndi was going to lose it and shank Tammy with a fork for the announcement.

However, Cyndi stoically calmed herself and sat. With what grace she could muster, she lined up the boat-load of tickets in a row on the tabletop. No one was allowed to touch them. With every basket number called, her shoulders tensed, and her eyes dropped from the announcer to the purple and blue tickets.

Gina leaned into me, her warm hand on my thigh where she gently squeezed. "She's nuts. I don't understand why she's checking to see if she won. All her tickets went into one basket."

Cyndi's head snapped around; her dark gaze narrowed on her sister. "I did too put tickets in other baskets—a few. I just want Jamison Blaine's the most." She then whirled her eyes back to Tammy. The hostess called out a number for one of four handmade quilts with books and authors' names stitched on the spines.

They were very cool. For someone like the Boba Book Babes, they would cherish it. But for me, it was nothing I would use daily—or at all.

All four Babes scanned their tickets to see if any of them won the prize. Gina bounced out of my embrace, raised her arms, and shouted, "Me!"

There were grumblings behind us. I turned my head and saw the Boozy Bitch blogger's group glaring at my girl. Their sour looks gave away their jealousy of Gina's winnings. I wanted to tell them to grow up, but what was the point? Sometimes, people fed off negativity. I wasn't going to add to the drama.

When Gina came back with the blanket cradled in her arms like a newborn baby, I had to smile at her. Her wide blue eyes sparkled with happiness, despite the shit show of this weekend.

"Now my weekend is almost complete," she admitted with a sigh. She sat, snuggled close to my side, and kissed my jaw. "You know what would complete my weekend?"

I met her eyes, which conveyed heat and wanting. Well, now, that perked up my dick immediately. "I—"

"I don't think so," Cyndi interrupted with a hiss. "I need you to stay. What if I don't win Jamison Blaine's basket?" Her crazed eyes bounced me with a warning. "Don't you dare take my sister away at this crucial moment."

"O-kay. I guess we'll wait to see who wins Jamison Blaine's basket." I surrendered.

My answer must have satisfied her, because Cyndi whipped back around and focused on the tickets again.

Finally, after thirty minutes, there were three more prizes left. The basket Cyndi wanted, a BDSM themed box from B.J. Dickson, and the final quilt. They raffled the blanket first, which Ricky from Boozy won. I've never seen a person cry so hard over a blanket before.

"Next basket is the B.J. Dickson's BDSM box." Tammy pulled a blue ticket out of the bag. "Winning ticket is..."

Silence rang out throughout the hall. Then a chirp came from Sam, which caught all of our attention.

"No way," Brandy huffed in disappointment. Then a big grin slowly creased her face. "Unless you won that for me."

Sam's eyes widened. "Umm..." She stood, a slight perspiration across her mocha skin. She glanced over at Brandy, and the tentative smile on Sam's face split into a huge grin. "Nope. This is for me." She then confidently walked toward the front and retrieved her winnings.

Brandy gasped and eyeballed her friend, all the while the rest of us chuckled. Once Sam took her seat again, her arms tight around the box full of different kinds of sex paraphernalia and two books.

"This is going to be fun," Sam uttered as she examined the contents of the box.

"You and I are going to have a chat back in the room later," Brandy sulked.

Tammy's voice cut through the quiet at our table. "Finally, here's the winning number for the Jamison Blaine's basket that's worth a small fortune. It has his entire male-male m-preg book series, uploaded on a brand new Kindle Fire. Along with the last book of that series coming out next month. There are two VIP tickets for the Silenced in San Antonio event, which I will also be attending," Tammy chortled out like that was important news. "And the most important part of the basket is an invitation to dinner with the author himself. Jamison Blaine. Now, isn't this an awesome prize?" The gleeful admission has me wondering if she, too, threw in tickets to win the basket.

"Stop blabbing and get on with it," Cyndi growled under her breath, but it was loud enough for the next table to hear.

"The winning number is... 543092. Purple ticket," Tammy belted out and then handed the ticket over to Izzy.

Tammy pulled out a slew of tickets from her pocket—almost as much as Cyndi bought—and scanned them.

Cyndi, who was frantically searching her tickets, paused, her finger on a purple ticket. Her body stiffened like if she moved she'd break into pieces.

"Cyndi?" Gina reached out and touched her sister's arm, pulling Cyndi out of her trance.

"I didn't win," she muttered, her eyes glazed in a watery haze.

"What?" Sam asked with a bit of worry. "That's not possible. Look at all those tickets."

"I didn't win," she repeated. Cyndi's voice was broken.

"Damn it," Brandy uttered, reaching out for her friend.

"Don't." Cyndi shook off her hand. "I'm good." But she

didn't look good. One touch, and I knew Gina's sister would break into a million pieces, or cry a million tears.

"Oh, girl," Sam said as she walked around and drew Cyndi into a hug, not caring if her friend wanted to be left alone.

In the short time I have spent with these women, I've learned, even though they were snarky and pushed each other's buttons, they cared for one another. It showed in their laughter, the smiles, and easy banter. The close friendship amongst the four Boba Book Babes was forged by love of books and boba tea—which, by the way, I never tried. But I'd rectify that real soon, with Gina.

Gina reached out and gripped her sister's hand.

"It's okay. It's only a basket," Cyndi muttered tightly.

"Last call." Izzy waved the ticket in the air.

"Well–well, I guess whoever's ticket this is lost out," Tammy announced with exuberance a minute later.

"You get another chance," Sam said, releasing Cyndi from her hug, and sat back down.

Tammy grabbed the bag from the volunteer and pulled out another ticket. "This time the ticket is blue. 543389."

Quiet descended the large room as everyone was looking over their tickets.

Then a loud, sucked-in gasp from Cyndi resonated throughout the quiet space. Gina and I simultaneously turn our heads toward her sister. Pure joy shined from her brown eyes.

"I won," she said, softly at first. "I won," she shouted this time.

"No surprise to me. You bought a crap-ton of tickets. I knew you'd win," Brandy laughed, her hand raised for a high five, which Cyndi promptly returned.

"Cyndi, call it out," Gina encouraged.

She nodded at Gina, then she jumped up and screamed, "Me!"

"Not those Boba Babes again," came from behind us.

More unhappy groans from behind as Cyndi hugged each of us, then she shot a finger at the Boozy Book Bitches. She then literally bounced herself up to the table, where Tammy's face twisted in a bitter frown, then flashed into a patronizing grin. Words were exchanged, but my attention swiftly shifted to the woman in my arms.

"I think it's time we escape into our own happy place." Gina waggled her brows and then stood. Her free hand took mine, tugging me from the chair.

Hmm. I'm happy to oblige my woman.

Before we left, Gina leaned over and whispered something to Brandy and gave her the blanket. Avoiding cheesy footprints and hotel employees scrubbing the floor, I followed Gina out of the event room.

Even before my feet halted, my hand slapped the up button for the elevator. The door slid open right away, and we got in. The moment I hit seven, Gina was on me.

Her red lips parted, and I took instant advantage. She tasted of wine, rich and addicting. She pulled the hem of my shirt out, and her fingers trailed along my stomach. Those light touches sent rivulets of desire through my veins.

I cupped her face, deepening the kiss. Then, one by one, I freed her ponytails so I could run my fingers through her beautiful hair. "Gina," I said into a kiss.

"I can't wait any longer, Philly." The passion in her eyes and the tone of her voice did it for me. Gina was the one who got away, but now, I wouldn't make the same mistakes like my mother made in her life.

The second the elevator opened onto my floor, I

scooped her up and carried her to my door. Gina had my key, and with a quick swipe over the lock, we were in.

There was no hesitation. No need to get to know each other. We knew each other more than most couples in a long-term relationship. I wanted that with her. Yes. I said it. I wanted to be with Gina in all manners, and I would move to Ohio for her, just to have her in my life forever.

"You're thinking too hard. Did you change your mind?"

Shit. I didn't realize I had stopped touching her.

With a gentle caress of her face, I crowded her to the bed. "I was thinking maybe Ohio is the place for me."

"Really? You would do that for me?"

I leaned down and took her mouth for a long, sultry kiss as though it was the answer to her questions. "Yes, Gina. I'd do anything for you."

"Oh, Phillip Austin Blackmoor, take me to bed and claim me as yours." As dramatic as Gina sounded, I do anything to make her happy.

Without another word, I kissed her. My hunger had no boundaries where this woman was concerned. Gina got my cue and stripped out of her Dorothy costume, and I yanked my shirt and jeans off, leaving me only in boxers.

My entire body froze when Gina stood in front of me in a matching ruby red, sparkly bra and panty set. She did a slow turn around, exposing her ass cheeks in the small thong, and my underwear couldn't contain the bulge. Or the need that was driving me to take her right there. But I remained steadfast.

"What do you think?"

"Jesus, woman. You're out to kill me." I appreciated every dip and curve of her beautiful body. More so, I appreciated Gina for who she was. Smart, talented, wicked sense of humor, and a beautiful soul. However, my dick wanted her intimately.

"Not my intention to kill you, but to do dirty things to you." She waggled her eyebrows. The pink tip of her tongue stuck out a bit. I groaned in anticipation.

"Well, you're doing something—now come here." I pulled her close, captured her mouth, and we both fell into bed.

"Ooh, Philly, is that a banana in your boxers or are you happy to see me?" Gina pressed her hips up and ground her pelvis against my hard length. I groaned.

"Always funny. Now show me what you can do with that smart mouth of yours. Kiss me," I ordered lightly. And she did.

Memorizing every inch of her flesh, I caressed her until her kisses went from soft to demanding. I unclasped her bra with a flick, exposing the bounty of her breasts to me.

"Gorgeous," I let out before taking a tight pink nipple into my mouth. I sucked and laved until she squirmed under me. Then I did the same to the other, giving equal attention.

"Ph—"

Before she finished my name, my fingers dipped into her lace-trimmed panties and I touched her wet heat. "Baby," I groaned, slipping a finger between her slick folds. "You're so slick for me. I need to taste you."

Gina let out a moan that went straight to my balls.

I released her breast and moved until my eyes were level with her thong. "You are intoxicating." I leaned in, pressing my face tight against the fabric. The smell of my woman drove me wild. My mouth watered. I had to have her on my tongue.

Without hesitating, I pulled down the tiny piece of

fabric. Once the material was free and clear of her limbs, I spread her legs wide and delved in like a starving man at a banquet.

It wasn't long before Gina sat up quickly, grabbing a fist of my long hair and pulling me face to face.

"Philly. As much as I want your mouth on me, I want you inside far more. Don't make me wait."

"Yes, ma'am." Then I kissed her, deep, wet—until she was extra needy. My fingers delved into her heat, stretching her until she was ready for me. I got out of bed, dropped my boxers, and retrieved the condom from my wallet. Once I quickly sheathed myself, I was between her spread legs. "I don't want to hurt you, so I'm going to take it slow."

"Okay." Gina licked her lips. "But not too slow."

She had no idea what that little bit of tongue did to me. I wanted to plunge in fast and hard to claim what was mine. Instead, I put my tip at her entrance and gently pushed.

"I don't know what makes my body hum more, the anticipation of you making love to me or the stretch and burn of your steely length burrowing inside me," Gina said sexily while her hands roved over my chest, tweaking my nipples.

"Dirty-talking Gina. I love that." I took possession of her mouth and slowly drove myself inside her until I was to the hilt. With a careful, easy glide, I plunged back inside her. Over and over, my hips were a steady rhythm as my mouth devoured hers.

"Baby," I said against her lips. "I'm never letting you go."

"Harder. Faster, Philly," Gina countered, her legs wrapped around my hips and her nails scored across my shoulder blades.

I did as I was told and fucked my woman hard and fast until she cried out my name.

Gina's climax had her shuttering under me. It wasn't long before that familiar sizzle in my balls had me careen over the edge. My entire body was a live wire. Every movement sent a jolt of electricity to my dick, which was still inside her.

I lifted my head and stared dazedly into Gina's eyes. Remnants of lust, satisfaction, and something else glazed her pupils. "Are you okay? Was I too rough?" Asking these questions was stupid, but I wanted the assurance I didn't hurt her.

She took my face with both hands and pulled me in for a sweet kiss. "No, Philly. It was perfect. You're perfect."

"I'll be gentler next time," I promised.

Gina's eyes hardened before they softened. "Seriously, Austin. It was great. I like it just how you gave it to me. So, don't go changing your ways. Okay?"

I couldn't help but smile. "Okay," I said, kissing the tip of her nose.

There was a beat of silence between us before I got up to rid myself of the condom and brought back a warm washcloth for Gina. Once we cleaned up, we nestled back in bed. We talked about our future and finally fell asleep in each other's arms, dreaming about the life we both were about to share.

Epilogue
Gina

Three months later...

A clanging bell jumpstarted Gina's heart. A moment later, the luggage carousel jerked to a start. Travelers crowded around the small opening, waiting for their baggage to be vomited out.

A familiar face caught Gina's attention, but she only saw the side profile for a second before Brandy diverted her with a gleeful retort.

"I hope mine comes first," she said while adjusting her headband.

"I don't. I hope it's last." Gina recalled the oversized red hard-sided suitcase covered in various authors' and funny stickers, like a "suck my balls" boba tea cup. The placement of the stickers formed the outline of a huge peen.

"No, you don't. Remember all the laughs watching the guys turn red as they read all the sayings? That reminds me. I'm going to video the crowd this time." Brandy plucked her phone out of her carry-on boba tea-shaped backpack and began recording.

Gina rolled her eyes, then pulled out her own phone. She sent a text to Austin. *We've landed. Waiting for our luggage.*

Austin immediately responded with a smiley and thumbs-up emoji, which put a smile on her face. They'd talked and made love the entire evening last night. Although Gina's heart already ached at their separation, it wasn't like Austin didn't live with her. He jumped at the chance when she asked him to move in with her two months ago. She was ecstatic at the life they planned to make together. They had been together ever since. A few days apart would be good for them.

Since Austin started a new job in the Cincinnati area the month before, he had requested the weekend off to attend the Silenced in San Antonio author event. He'd catch the red-eye Saturday morning and arrive at the hotel before the Boba Book Babes had breakfast. With that thought, her heart ached a little less.

Gina hoped her sister Cyndi would be as happy as she was one day.

"Crap. I just got Sam's message. Their flight was delayed," Brandy called from over her shoulder. "But sometimes the pilots make it up in the air."

"We can hope. I'll check the arrivals." Gina gestured to a row of monitors hanging on the wall. "Keep a lookout for my bag."

"Will do." Brandy gave her a salute and pointed the phone toward businessmen, who were probably waiting for their golf bags.

Gina scanned the flight numbers until she found 2063.

She rechecked Cyndi's message and found the arrival time was only fifteen minutes behind schedule.

She returned to Brandy's side. "We've got about an hour before they get here. There's my suitcase." Gina squeezed through the crowd and plucked her gray bag from the conveyor. She set it upright and extended the handle. The shell of her bag had several bookish stickers, but, unlike Brandy's, hers weren't arranged as male genitalia.

The "books are lit" and "just one more chapter" stickers were colorful and useful in distinguishing her bag from the other boring gray suitcases. She rolled over to Brandy just as her friend giggled.

"Look." Brandy held up her phone, ready to catch the scene. Her giant red suitcase, packed with her book harness and other fabulous items like her new Boba Book Babes shirt, spewed from the opening.

A small group of women, comfortably dressed in what appeared to be fleece pajamas, pointed toward the red behemoth and laughed. One even took a photo.

"I wonder if they are going to the book event?" Gina asked, studying their faces.

"I hope they aren't the Texas branch of the Boozy Book Bitches," Brandy continued recording as the bag closed in on their position.

"Maybe they just like books," Gina surmised.

"Or dick." Brandy smirked.

"Brandy!" Gina nudged her friend in the side.

"Well? It could be." She shrugged. "Why are you blushing? You like it too. That big ol' book boyfriend wanker of Austin's."

"Oh my God." Gina covered her face while shaking her head. She had to admit Brandy was right. She loved Austin's body and how it made her feel. Austin's anatomy was her private playground, and she wasn't about to spill the details to her best friend.

Brandy laughed as she retrieved her luggage. "You are as red as my suitcase."

Ignoring her friend, Gina surveyed the broad area. "Let's head to the café and get some coffee while we wait for Cyndi and Sam."

They ordered their drinks and took a seat near the entrance. As they sipped their iced lattes, Brandy scrolled through her phone.

"Crap. There's a news post about Molly."

"Really? What does it say?" Gina asked, taking another sip of her drink.

"We knew she was denied bail. But her trial for both murders is set for January."

"I don't know why they are waiting until January. She confessed she killed Rodney and Chad," she said with a frown.

Gina leaned back in her seat and closed her eyes for a second. The memory from three months ago was still fresh in her mind. How Molly fessed up to those murders and her convoluted reason for killing those men was ridiculous.

"Well, I hope they throw the book at her. Though, some professionals on twitter are saying the court might be lenient on her case because the murders weren't pre-meditated." Brandy's steely gaze met Gina's blue eyes. "And I'm not even joking."

"Whatever they do, she'll be locked up for a long time," Gina added.

"Let's change the subject to something fun." Brandy pulled out the map of the Silenced in San Antonio book event. "We get to see Duke Wain again," she said without her gaze straying away from the paper. "He's at table

twenty-three. I wonder if his westerns sell better in the west?"

"What else did you print out?" Gina asked, holding the cool cup.

"The itinerary." Brandy sighed and took a long swallow of her latte. "I've got the whole time planned. When the VIP hour opens, I'm starting in the back. Come hell or flooded River Walk, I'll get all my books signed this time."

"You got all your books signed at the Peoria event, too," Gina reminded, trying to remember the good things about that trip, like Austin's hands sliding over her body.

"Yeah, I know, but I have a system. And it was interrupted." Brandy folded the paper and stuffed it into her backpack.

"Murder will do that," Gina huffed.

"Here's to an uneventful event." Brandy raised her glass.

Gina bumped it with hers. "Here, here." She totally agreed on the uneventful aspect, except for Saturday night. Austin would be there to rock her world.

"I have an addendum." Brandy's grin morphed into a mischievous smirk. "The only eventful allowance will be allotted to Cyndi. I hope she and the object of her masturbation can get it on."

Gina nearly spat out vanilla latte. "Me too," she giggled.

Her phone pinged, and she woke the screen. "Cyndi and Sam have arrived. They're disembarking."

"Let's go. I'm ready to tease Cyndi." Brandy wadded up a napkin.

They returned to the baggage claim and waited near the hallway, hoping to spot Sam and Cyndi. As the crowd of people filtered by, Brandy raised her hand and waved.

Gina saw Sam first. Nearly a head taller than Cyndi, Sam rocked her cowgirl boots.

"Do you have it?" Brandy asked as Cyndi came close.

"Of course." Gina shifted from side to side with a grin. She reached inside her carry-on and pulled out a neon pink gift sack. White crepe paper stuck out of the bag, hiding the gift.

She and Brandy had schemed a way to reward and yet embarrass Cyndi since she'd won the Jamison Blaine prize at Pandemonium in Peoria. It's the only thing her sister would talk about.

Gina's gaze panned the area, then snapped back to her sister. She raised her middle finger in a salute. "Welcome to San Antonio."

"Best greeting ever." With a wide grin, Cyndi pulled Gina into a fierce hug.

Over Cyndi's shoulder, Gina met Sam's gaze. "Somebody is happy."

Sam rolled her eyes. "We didn't need a plane to get here. She's walking on cloud nine."

Gina enjoyed the moment in her sister's embrace. Cyndi's excitement and joy were contagious.

Having Jamison personalize and sign her books had been on Cyndi's bucket list, but now she had the opportunity to converse with the bestselling author one on one.

"Are you ready to meet him?" Brandy asked. "How many batteries did you drain these last three months?"

Cyndi giggled like a schoolgirl. "You don't need batteries anymore. You need to get a rechargeable, girl."

Brandy rested a hand on her waist as she cocked her hip to the side. "Don't worry about me." She winked.

"Yes. Don't worry about Brandy. She brought her handcuffs," Gina teased.

Brandy blushed, but her smile widened. "Gina has a gift for you, Cyndi. It's in honor of Jamison Blaine."

"Lube?" Sam asked, grinning.

Gina held up the bag and offered it to Cyndi. They moved toward the side, out of the way, as the bell announced the start of the luggage carousel.

Cyndi took the bag and shook it. "What is it?"

"You won't know until you open it, silly." Sam tapped her booted foot. She tried to peek inside the bag.

Her sister removed the paper and stuffed her hand inside it. She pulled out a pale-yellow shirt. Sam held the empty bag while Cyndi unfolded the soft fabric. A little blue boba tea character held hands with a pink boba tea. "Jamison Blaine's Boba Book Babe," she read, then glanced at Gina.

"Really?" A bright smile illuminated Cyndi's face. She flipped the shirt over and rested it against her body, checking the fit. "I love it."

For Gina, meeting Austin again had been a dream come true. Now it was Cyndi's turn to find her happily ever after.

The End... For Now

Letter to the Reader

Dear Reader,

Once upon a time... there were two romance authors who had tables next to each other at a book signing. They laughed, sold some books, and (lovingly) flipped each other off. And that's how CJ and Rochelle became besties.

Thank you so much for reading Pandemonium in Peoria, book 1 of the Boba Book Babes Mysteries. We hope you enjoyed it. But there's more to come. So, watch out world there are five Boba Book Babes Mysteries novels planned.

What's coming next? Silenced in San Antonio. It's a thrilling romantic mystery where Cyndi DiCaprio discovered there's more than meets the eye of her favorite author. Will she and the BBB get embroiled in another murder mystery at the event? You would have to wait for that answer!

Speaking of love, please return some, and leave a review. We would truly appreciate it.

Smooches,

CJ & Rochelle

Boba Book Babes Mysteries 2
Silenced in San Antonio teaser:

The second I stepped foot outside of the San Antonio International Airport, a warm breeze swept across my face. I glanced down at my watch, which read five forty-eight pm. I tipped my head back for a second and closed my eyes, enjoying the seventy degrees plus weather while regrouping my excitement for the impending date with Jamison Blaine.

He was my favorite author of all time and his long running thirty-four book male-male m-preg series had been my number one read from the second I picked up the first book, *Running Wild*.

"Cyndi, are you still with us?" I heard my twin saying.

I popped my eyes open and glanced at her. Her bright blue eyes honed in on my face. "What? Can't a girl enjoy the day?" I snarked out.

"Sure, but not at the expense of getting your ass ran over by an Uber driver," Brandy bit out.

I glanced around and, sure enough, I was standing partially out on the street where the car pulled up for their pick up. "Oops. Sorry." I scrunched up my nose at the oncoming cab driver, who ended up flipping me off.

"Asshole," I called out and gave him the middle finger.

"Hey, I thought that was only reserved for me?" Gina chuckled.

"No. But I do offer you a double sometimes," I countered with a smirk.

"Babes, the ride is here," Sam called out and waved us over to the minivan. An older man slid out of the driver's seat and opened the trunk. One by one, he put our luggage in the back while we piled in the seats.

My phone pinged with a text as I just sat down at the very back. I took out my phone where an unknown number showed. I swiped the screen and the top part of the message read, Hi it's me.

Well, that was weird.

I opened up the message fully and my heart nearly jumped out of the chest. I must have wheezed out a breath, because three heads turned my way.

"What is it?" Gina asked.

"Did you get a dick pic?" Brandy waggled her eyebrows.

"Is it work?" Sam added as she stretched over next to me to read the message. She too sucked in a breath when she saw who the text came from. "Oh, my."

I met her eyes before I utter, "Jamison Blaine just messaged me."

"What?" Gina and Brandy said at the same time.

I nodded vigorously like some crazed bobble head. "Yeah."

"Well?" Brandy pushed.

"Read it," Gina insisted.

I took another breath in and blew it out. "Jamison said

that he wants me to come to his suite once I arrive at the hotel. He wants to meet me first and talk before we head for dinner. Room 1764. Floor seventeen. And now I have his number, so I can text him back." I could scream with excitement. Meeting my favorite author was exciting enough, but the idea of going out to dinner with the gorgeous man was down right mind-blowing to me.

"I'm so jealous," Brandy muttered under her breath. "Maybe it'll be more than a get-to-know-you meeting." She winked.

"Is that all you think about?" I asked with a chuckle.

"Only fifty percent of the time," Brandy said in all seriousness.

"Okay, ladies. The Rio Grande Hotel on the Riverwalk?" the driver asked as he adjusted the rearview mirror.

We all chirped at the same time, "Yes."

Not fifteen minutes later, we pulled up to the hotel. The driver hustled out of the minivan. The hotel porter grabbed our luggage and put them on the trolley. While Gina checked us in, I finally texted Jamison back.

Me: Hi Jamison. We just arrived at the hotel. Please give me ten min.

All I got was crickets for the next few minutes as we headed up to the elevator on the twelfth floor. The moment we entered the adjoining rooms, my phone went off with another text.

I froze, nervous enthusiasm coursing through my veins. I was going to meet Jamison Blaine. A New York Times and USA best-selling author was going to have dinner with me. I still couldn't fathom that.

I quickly glanced at the message, squealed, and immediately changed into my outfit. A black baby-doll dress with three-quarter sleeves, black Louboutin pumps, I got for a steel online. Ran into the bathroom and added some makeup on my face and stepped out of the room. My sister was standing by the bed, arms folded across her chest, and her eyes scanning me.

"What did the man say?" Gina walked over and nudged me with her hip.

I could tell she wanted to take my phone out of my hands, but I quickly drew it close to my chest.

"He told me to come up whenever I'm ready," I confessed. Then my zeal petered out. "Gina?"

My twin looked at me with worry creasing her mouth. "What's wrong?"

"What if he doesn't like me?" I hated the way my voice sounded small.

"Really? My sister, who usually has an I-don't-give-a-hoot-about-what-anyone-thinks attitude is worried about a man liking her? Cyndi, just have fun. Besides, it's not like it's an actual date."

"Technically, it is," Sam jumped in as she swung the door open between our adjoining rooms.

"I mean—oh, shit. You look hot." Brandy waved a hand over her face. "You're going to eat him alive... if he's lucky."

That made me laugh. "Thanks. I needed that." Glancing at myself once more in the mirror by the door, I ignored my sister's comment about a real date. "I'll text you the 9-1 1 if it doesn't go well."

"You'll have a good time. But you should text us where you're going, just in case," Brandy added.

"Good idea." With another wave, I headed to the seventeenth floor.

Jello-legged, I took another long, even breath to strengthen my confidence and knocked on the door.

Not a second later, the door swung open and Jamison

stood there, all smiles. My excitement geared up again, and I couldn't help plastering a huge smile on my face. This man was a dream.

Jamison took a good, long look at me. For a second, I wanted to step back, but he met my eyes and smiled. Then it was my turn to get a good look at the man I'm going to dinner with and realized I had totally overdressed.

He had on a pair of tight blue jeans, knees purposely torn, and a clingy Van Halen T-shirt. The man was gorgeous. He had dark blue eyes, thick black lashes, which matched the short raven hair. He didn't wear his geeky black glasses I normally saw on him, or the collared shirt with his signature bow tie, but he was...

"You're smoking hot. Come in, Sandy."

"Um... My name is Cyndi." My stomach dropped from his error.

Then I really took a good look at his face. "Wait..."

"Want some wine?" he interrupted. "We have a great vintage that will blow your socks off," he offered as he went to the mini fridge and pulled out a shorty.

"Um, no thank you." I kept staring at him until it hit me. "You're not Jamison Blaine."

He stopped mid-step and turned to me, eyes narrowed on my face. "What makes you say that?"

"First, I never saw Jamison dressed this shabby. Then, since his eyesight is bad, he can't get Lasik. So, he wears those cute, fashionable glasses that makes his... never mind. Your nose is crooked too." I then snapped my mouth shut, because I sound like a crazed fan.

Because you are.

"Stalk much?" Fake Jamison said.

"Who are you?" I demanded, with narrowing eyes.

"He's my assistant." A deep voice came from the bedroom.

Right then, the real Jamison Blaine walked out. His beautiful black hair brushed back, black-rimmed glasses on, with his signature bow around his neck, and a beguiling smile on his face. "Hi, Cyndi."

About the Rochelle

Rochelle Bradley puts an artistic spin on everything she does but there are two things she fails at miserably:
1. Cooking (seriously, she can burn water)
2. Sewing (buttons immediately fall back off)
She loves baking and makes a mean BTS (Better than Sex) cake. When in observation mode she is quiet, however, her mouth is usually open with an encouraging glass-is-half-full pun or, quite possibly, her foot.
She's a Bearcat, a Buckeye, an interior decorator, and fluent in sarcasm.
Rochelle shares her home with two kitties, her daughter, her son, and her Prince.
She loves to connect with readers and show off her cats or new book news. You can find her on Facebook, Twitter, Pinterest, YouTube, TikTok, and Instagram.
Visit Rochelle's website to sign up for her newsletter to keep up to date about future novels and book signings (RochelleBradley.com).

About CJ Warrant

Award-Winning Author CJ Warrant was born an overseas Army brat, in a Korean Italian household, but settled in the states at five. With a career in the beauty industry, married to a wonderful supportive man, three grown kids and new cat mom, her view of life is as such. Life is a journey; both good and bad, light to the dark. She takes it all in, learns from every experience and captures those moments in her stories.

Want to know more about CJ's books, upcoming events and books coming up, then stalk her!
www.cjwarrant.com/newsletter
CJ's Coven
https://www.facebook.com/groups/167874440806362
CJ's M/M Coven
https://www.facebook.com/groups/473999584518439
www.facebook.com/cjwarrant/
https://www.bookbub.com/profile/cj-warrant
www.twitter.com/cjwarrant
www.instagram.com/cjwarrant/
www.pinterest.com/cjwarrant/
www.goodreads.com/cjwarrant/
https://www.amazon.com/CJ-Warrant/e/B01BTK1T40

Books by Rochelle

By Rochelle K. Bradley

Secrets of the Fallen

Descended

Awakened

Enlightened

Dragons of Ellehcor Fairy Tale Retellings

Dragonfly Wishes

Dragunzel

Books by Rochelle Bradley

The Fortuna, Texas Series

The Double D Ranch

Plumb Twisted

More Than a Fantasy

Municipal Liaisons

Here We Go Again

The Playboy's Pretend Fiancée

Cole's New Song

The Fortuna Dare Society

Brad

Jasen (Municipal Liaisons)

Canon

Forrest

Parker

B.J.

Books By CJ Warrant

Contemporary Romance

Sweet Reunion

Sweet Redemption

Dark Supernatural Thriller

Forgetting Jane

Dance of the Mourning Cloak

Dark Erotic Thriller

Mirror Image

A Chance At Love Novella MM Romance Series

Four Days

One Kiss

Five Seasons of Love

Two Of Hearts

Saints vs Sinners Series

Deacon – Book 1

Coming Later 2022-2023

Three Times Lucky – Book 4 of A Chance At Love Series
Sweet Little Valentines – Landry Brothers Duet Short
Kyle – Book 2 from the Saints vs Sinners Series

Made in the USA
Middletown, DE
27 June 2022

67690983R00129